SWEET STRIPES

SWEET STRIPES

WHITETIDE STREAK BOOK TWO

MARIE LONG

Sweet Stripes
(The Whitetide Streak, Book 2)

Copyright © 2024 by Marie Long
Published by Chikara Press

Cover by Jacqueline Sweet Design

Printed in the United States of America

10 9 8 7 6 5 4 3 2 1

ISBN: 978-1-960253-07-1 (paperback)
ISBN: 978-1-960253-06-4 (eBook)

SWEET STRIPES

PROLOGUE

The serene morning ambience of Hunter's Rest was shattered by the cacophony of two tigers battling. The angry growls and snarls echoed off the distant oaks, sending crows squawking off in their obnoxious alarm.

Gauge Reed pinned his younger sister to the ground, digging his claws into her front and hind legs. His inner tiger seethed. After six long months of avoiding the last remaining family he knew, Gauge had not been expecting this kind of reunion. Cammy Reed was still a cub at heart, but she was a mysterious woman. She was always up to something even when she didn't appear to be. She had her own motives, which was why Gauge was baffled at finding her here in Diesel's territory.

Cammy didn't fight back, not that she could, as Gauge bore his muscular four-hundred-pound weight down on her. She simply glared at him, her orange-gold tiger's eyes staring deep into his soul. She projected a telepathic message to his mind.

"Hello, Furball."

Gauge let out an agitated roar. He'd always despised that ridiculous nickname. *"Call me that again, and I'll tear out your fucking throat."*

Cammy roared back. *"You do that, and Diesel will come after your ass. You're trespassing in his territory."*

The mention of their older brother's name piqued his interest. Having returned from his long journey of training and finding himself, he was hoping to see Diesel again and face him in battle. Gauge had lost to him once before, but this time, he was more prepared. He had decided to do it stealthily, with his fur covered in mud and leaves to mask his scent in hopes of getting a preemptive strike on his brother.

"Where is he?" Gauge projected the question into his sister's mind.

Cammy sneered. *"I'm not telling you shit. Get out of here now."*

"Not until I see him."

"You'll have to kill me first in order to see him."

Gauge bared his canines. He raised his left paw, claws extended, and stared at her exposed throat.

She lifted her head slightly, giving him easier access.

He blinked. *She's willing to die for that bastard?* His paw shook as he wrestled with his thoughts.

"How can you protect him after what he's done to our family?" Gauge asked her telepathically.

"He did nothing to our family, and you know it," Cammy projected. *"You're just upset he couldn't defeat Axle... And neither could you, apparently."*

A low growl rumbled in his throat. Axle Reed, their eldest brother, was the current alpha of the Whitetide Streak—or what was left of it. He was a disgrace of a leader, yet nobody had been able to take the throne. The more Gauge thought about the situation, the more helpless he felt. As strong as Diesel was, Gauge couldn't persuade him to take over. Diesel wanted no part of the clan now. Gauge had nowhere else to turn to—no family, no mate... He was truly alone.

At last, Gauge retracted his claws and tore his gaze from Cammy's throat. Killing his sister wouldn't fix the shit with Axle. And he also didn't need to deal with Diesel's wrath. He moved off her and sat nearby, looking at her.

"I didn't come here to kill you," he projected into her mind.

Cammy rolled onto her belly and licked the small claw wounds on her front paws. *"You've got balls, coming here at all,"* she replied, not looking at him.

He closed his eyes for a moment then sighed deeply through his nose. *"Why are you keeping him away from me?"*

Cammy stopped licking her paw and glowered at him. *"Because I don't trust you. Especially after what you did before, trying to steal his mate just to coerce him to fight. You're pathetic, Gauge."*

"I never intended to steal his mate for myself. I only did it to test him. To see if after all those years of him being away, he would have the drive and strength to finally defeat Axle."

Gauge recalled that fateful night he and Diesel fought. He'd regretted it ever since. Diesel was more than ready. But it seemed useless to implore his help now. Diesel had other obligations.

"It was shitty all around. You're a dick. Go back to Greyson Creek where you belong," Cammy projected.

Gauge hung his head and stood. This was proving to be a losing battle. Cammy was headstrong, and as much as he hated her for it, he didn't have the guts to harm her just to get his way. But going back home wouldn't be easy. And just defeating Axle wouldn't solve the Whitetide Streak's long-term problems either.

His tail lashed back and forth, echoing his nervousness. *"I can't go back."*

Cammy tilted her head, regarding him curiously. *"And why the hell not?"*

"Because even if I manage to defeat Axle myself, I can't guarantee the Whitetide Streak will be able to sustain itself."

She perked up. *"What do you mean?"*

Gauge snarled. He sensed the conversation taking an undesirable turn. Since he couldn't make amends with his brothers, Gauge was left with one last alternative, one last hope for redeeming his dignity: finding a mate. But that outlook seemed bleak. *What worthy mate would want a clan outcast?*

When he didn't respond, Cammy snorted mockingly. *"Oh... I see. So that's what it's* really *about,"* she continued.

Gauge cast her a befuddled stare. *"What?"*

"Don't play dumb. I know that look. And I can smell your fear. Embarrassment… You're looking for a mate. That's why you really came to New Rochford, wasn't it? It had nothing to do with Diesel."

Although she'd seemed dense, Cammy was as sharp as a knife. She appeared to know more about him than he knew about himself. *"It had everything to do with him,"* he replied, trying to convince himself more than her. *"He has to take the throne."*

"That throne has been tainted ever since Axle came to power. Diesel doesn't want it, and I don't blame him."

Gauge dug his claws into the dirt, exasperated. He was running out of options—running out of excuses.

"Tell the truth," Cammy continued, staring at him intently. *"It's a mate you want. But you're too chickenshit to admit it."*

He sneered. *That brat…* Then his mind wandered, and he thought about the possibility of a mate—a plump female he could sink his claws into. *"Even if it was what I wanted, I would never be happy, as long as Axle was in charge,"* he projected to his sister.

"Then why don't you take the throne?"

He swallowed once.

Axle had soiled the Whitetide family name, making countless enemies. After Gauge failed to defeat his eldest brother in battle, he attempted to entice Diesel to fight Axle, but that plan had proved to be his biggest mistake. Gauge's multiple failures indicated he was far from ready to take the throne, but he also couldn't endure another day living under Axle's rule.

When Gauge didn't respond, Cammy shook her head, turned, and trekked toward a narrow path leading deeper into the forest. *"I'm done with you."*

Gauge watched her for a moment as he let his mind wander. His life really was pathetic. He lacked the confidence in himself that he wouldn't fail a third time. To face Axle again—and lose—would surely mean death. But he didn't want to die alone. Just once, he wanted to feel what it was like to be accepted and loved unconditionally. And he would get that only from his one true mate. The more Gauge thought about Cammy's suggestion in taking the throne as Alpha of the Whitetide Streak, the more he realized that maybe that was something he'd secretly desired all along. For Diesel, who had willingly given up that opportunity as if it were an insignificant piece of lint, the position was practically destined for him, while Gauge was left struggling to carve out his own destiny. Being the youngest brother meant life tended to deal him the worst cards from the deck.

Gauge took a deep breath, shook off the muddy mess of leaves from his fur as best he could, and rushed after Cammy. His head held low, he caught up to her and walked a short distance behind her. *"Okay…"* he projected to his sister. *"You're right. I want a mate… and maybe I do want the throne. But I don't know where or how to start. I have nobody in my corner…"*

Cammy stopped walking and slowly looked over her shoulder. She let out an amused growl. *"Are my ears deceiving me, or did you just admit that I'm right? You* never *admit that I'm right!"* she replied in his mind.

He sighed. *"Look, are you going to help me or not?"*

"That depends on what kind of 'help' you're looking for. I'm sure as hell not going to fight your battles. You need to decide what you want for yourself."

"I want a mate. I want a family. I want my clan back."

"You sure about that? I don't think you're ready, if you ask me."

"Well, I didn't ask you."

She stared at him long and hard then gave a subtle head gesture for him to follow. Afterward, she continued along the forest path.

His head inclined, Gauge walked beside her. A small part of him was grateful that his sister was sparing him the time, though his pride was cut deep. He wasn't sure what he would say to Diesel if he saw him again. After all, Gauge used Diesel's mate as bait in order to get Diesel riled up enough to fight Axle. But when that plan backfired, Gauge and Diesel's estranged relationship had gone beyond simple apologies.

They reached a clearing where a small cabin sat. Cammy went to the back of the cabin, to an attached porch. She shifted back to her human form, a lithe, athletic, twenty-four-year-old woman with long golden hair and smooth, olive-toned skin. She grabbed a beach towel sitting on a shelf on the porch and wrapped it around her nude body.

Gauge respectfully averted his gaze and assessed the cabin's exterior. *Is this your place or Diesel's?* he inquired in her mind.

Cammy spun and faced him. "It's D's," she replied aloud. "Stay here a moment. I need to check on the cubs."

Cubs? he thought, watching her disappear inside the cabin. Gauge never thought of her as the intimate type, and she'd vocally expressed how much she'd never wanted a mate or cubs. Perhaps she'd finally changed her mind. That made Gauge feel even more pathetic about his own life. *Even that annoying little brat managed to settle down. What the fuck is wrong with me?*

Cammy soon returned fully dressed and cradling a small baby boy wrapped in a blue blanket while she fed him a bottle. A miniature brown canvas knapsack hung from her shoulder.

Gauge perked up. Faint black tiger stripes ran along the kid's arms and around the back of his neck. More stripes appeared to run down the baby's body, which was concealed by the blanket. He wouldn't be able to shift for several years, but the evidence of his manifesting powers was already beginning to reveal itself.

Gauge approached to get a better look at the baby.

Cammy shook her head. "Don't come any closer."

Her initial rejection left Gauge speechless for a moment. Then he inclined his head. *"Am I not allowed to see your kid?"* he projected into her mind.

She snorted out a laugh. *"My* kid? Ha! No. Are you crazy? This is D's son, Zahair. And I'm telling you to stay back so D doesn't smell your scent on him. The last thing I need is for him to rant and rave at me about why I had his cubs near you. It's bad enough I let you come this far, to his home. But this is as far as you go."

Gauge nodded slowly and stared at his nephew from afar. Zahair was lost in his own world while he happily sucked down milk from the bottle.

"Cubs? He has more?" he asked Cammy.

"He has a daughter, Indira. She's still sleeping. Carina, D's mate, is expecting again, so there will certainly be more on the way."

Sparks of anger, jealousy, and sadness ripped through Gauge's mind. Diesel had moved on from the past and started fresh, while Gauge continued to live his same stagnant life of frustration. But that life was all Gauge knew, and he wasn't sure where to go or what to do beyond the Whitetide Streak.

"I'll try to help you figure out your... little problem..." Cammy continued, pinning Gauge with a dubious look. "On one condition."

Gauge cocked his head.

"You don't drag D into any of this. Your problem is not his problem anymore. It's time you grew a pair and fought your own battles. If you want the damn throne, then for fuck's sake, take it. That's what Aunt Evaline would've said if she were here."

The thought of his late aunt Evaline, the former matriarch of the Whitetide Streak, drew a shiver down his spine that caused the fur on his back to rise. Listening to Cammy's words, he heard it in the tone of his late aunt come back from the dead. As disturbing as it was, a small part of him felt compelled to heed her advice.

"Okay, deal," he projected at last, lifting his head up to look at Cammy again.

Her narrowed golden eyes bore into him. "You *sure* you're ready for a mate?"

Gauge flicked his gaze at Zahair again, a constant reminder of what he'd always hoped for someday, then took a deep breath and replied telepathically, *"Yes, it's important to me."*

"Is it really what you *want*? Or what you feel *obligated* to do?"

He thought for a moment. *"Both?"*

"It won't matter either way if Axle kills you."

Gauge snarled. *"He won't, because I'm not going to lose. Not this time…"* But even as he projected those words to her, he thought about her warning. He wanted nothing more than to show his brothers he was capable of being an alpha, but deep inside, his lonely tiger also desired a mate. Living under Axle's tyranny, Gauge had never had the opportunity to meet someone special. Ironically, Axle himself couldn't keep a mate longer than a few days. As a result, the Whitetide Streak lacked heirs, and the pack's enemies knew it.

"I'm willing to risk my life for the chance that I can settle down with a mate," Gauge continued.

Cammy smirked. "Prove it."

He blinked. *"How the hell do I do that? I only have one shot against Axle. I haven't even been able to beat Diesel…"*

She watched Zahir finish his milk then took the bottle away and adjusted him in her arms. Zahir's big brown eyes stared up at the morning sky for a moment then swiveled toward Gauge. He cooed and gummed his tiny fist.

Gauge looked back at his nephew with trepidation. He wondered what was going on in the kid's mind. *What terrible things has Diesel already told his son about me?*

"I can't fight your battles, Gauge," Cammy continued. "I don't give two shits about the throne. But I know this means a lot to you, so… maybe you ought to come at this from a different angle."

"Such as?"

"Think about it, Furball. Axle has been making more enemies than friends. It's one of the main reasons why I got the hell out of there. Every day, there was a threat of war from some rival clan or another because Axle pissed somebody off. The Whitetide Streak had lost its respect. It's been a while since I've been back home, so I wonder what big-time rival clan Axle has gotten his ass mixed up with this time?"

Gauge thought. Axle had so many enemies that he'd lost count. Every day, they were fighting for their lives, living on the edge. They had fought many battles, keeping their enemies at bay for a little while, but Axle had failed to catch and kill a clan leader, which was an even greater embarrassment to the Whitetide Streak. Since his aunt's passing, Gauge had forgotten what peace really felt like. *"I see. So, if I were to somehow defeat the leader of one of these rival clans where Axle had failed to do so, then that could prove my worth as alpha."*

"Bingo. You think anyone would want to keep following Axle when you end up taking out the clan's greatest enemy and making peace? I sure the hell wouldn't. Now, we're done here. You better go before D returns. He won't be so generous with your presence as I have."

"I'm sure he will smell that I was here…"

"Yes, but I'll smooth things over so he doesn't go looking for you." She slid the canvas knapsack from her shoulder and tossed it at him. "Here."

Gauge sniffed at the bag curiously. *"What's this for?"*

"Seeing as you probably don't have any money, clothes, or food on you, it's a little something to keep you going."

If he could've smiled, he would have. *She really does care…* He'd been wandering alone for months, practically living off the land, and had avoided civilization for some time. Most of his money and valuables were still at Greyson Creek—if Axle hadn't sold or tossed them already. He also had a small setup in New Rochford where he'd opened an auto mechanic shop, which he'd later turned over to an old friend. The Whitetide Streak family had various types of investments throughout the world, which had, in turn, been split amongst the siblings. Gauge often tried to forget he had a shitload of money, because he'd preferred to live a quiet, stress-free life. He'd seen what money did to people in other clans, and he wanted no part of that corrupted life.

"Sorry, I couldn't find an extra toothbrush," she continued with a shrug.

"It's okay," Gauge projected to her. He picked up the bag with his jaws then shimmied his body through the straps, securing it around himself. *"Thanks, Sis…"*

"Mm-hmm. Now, go." She pointed.

Gauge backed away slowly, casting a look at his nephew for perhaps the last time. Then he stared at Cammy. His heart swelled, grateful for his little sister's counsel. She was truly the last person he thought would give him a second chance after the mistakes he'd made. Yet he still had some doubts about finding a mate. Gauge was damaged goods more than Diesel was. Happily-ever-afters were never meant for people like him. And even if he managed to get lucky, that happiness would most likely come with a steep price.

Gauge trekked in his tiger form almost a hundred miles through dense forests and across the vast open landscapes, back to Greyson Creek, a place he'd once called home. He'd walked all day, nonstop, and his paws were aching from the journey, but still, he pressed on. He used his solitude to plan his next move—to destroy his brother's enemies. But doing so would prove difficult alone. He, too, needed allies.

Nighttime was fast approaching. His muscles were sore, and he needed to replenish his energy for the next day. His shifter abilities gave him endurance and stamina that rivaled a jaguar's, but he'd pushed himself to the limit. With no inn or motel in sight, he would be forced to sleep under the stars that night.

A streetlight shone a bluish-white glow ahead through the trees. Gauge followed it like a beacon. He emerged from the forest and discovered the back of a midsized rickety-looking wooden house, where the source of the light was attached to a corner. He wandered around the side of the building and noticed a wood-chipped parking lot with one car parked. Then he peered around to the front of the building. A vintage sign hanging from an attached wrought-iron frame read General Store. Crates of fresh fruits and vegetables sat out in the front porch area, next to a pair of old rocking chairs.

Gauge let out a small sigh of relief, immediately recognizing this historic structure that reminded him of the old-time general stores of yesteryear. He was in Cedarstone Heights, a tiny rural town three miles wide and thirty miles south of Greyson Creek. He was almost home.

He slinked back behind the building, away from lights and people. Then he shimmied the canvas knapsack off his body and set it beside him. With a deep sigh, he plopped down on the grass. He groaned, feeling every throbbing muscle in his body. He closed his eyes, enjoying the peaceful solitude of night, but despite his body's exhaustion, he still found falling asleep difficult. His mind betrayed him, and he kept picturing the nightmare of his violent battles against Diesel and Axle long ago. The two battles that he could never win kept replaying over and over.

CHAPTER 1

How the hell did I let this happen? Aniyah Evans pored over the recipe for strawberry rosewater fondant. The mixture didn't look quite right. She'd made the fondant a hundred times for clients, and not once had she ever been short of ingredients.

She stared at her measuring teaspoon, which held only a few drops of the remaining rose water, and swore under her breath. The cake had to be finished and delivered to her client the next morning. Getting a special ingredient wasn't easy— the closest grocery store that carried her only trusted brand of rose water was over an hour away. She glanced at the stove's clock. She could make it to the store five minutes before closing time if she booked it.

She picked up her cell phone and dialed Ron's General Store.

"Afternoon, Ms. Evans," Ron Frawley, the owner, answered.

Aniyah smiled at his cute country drawl. "Hi, Ron. Listen, I have a bit of an emergency here. Think you can do me a little favor?"

"Of course. Name it."

Aniyah took a deep breath. "I need some more Niagua-brand rose water ASAP. Can you *please* keep the store open a little longer until I get there?"

A brief pause cinched the other end of the line. "That's a pretty steep favor, Ms. Evans. I gotta be somewhere later tonight."

Aniyah bit her bottom lip. She hated asking Ron for favors, especially since he'd done so much for her, giving her special discounts for driving so far to shop at his store. But her baking emergency made her desperate. "Please, Ron. I wouldn't be asking you if it wasn't important. I'll pay the full price, plus extra."

"No, no. Don't worry 'bout that. Come on by."

She breathed a sigh of relief. "Thanks, Ron. You're the best. I'll bake you the biggest pan of banana nut bread for this."

Ron chuckled. "I'm lookin' forward to it."

She ended the call and rushed to her bedroom to grab her purse. As she fumbled for her keys, the phone beeped with a notification. She scrambled back to the kitchen and grabbed it from the counter. A notification ribbon from her Plenti of Dates app flashed on the screen and read, *You have 1 new admirer!*

Aniyah wrinkled her nose sourly. *I thought I deleted that stupid app months ago,* she thought. After numerous failed attempts with matchmaking sites and apps, dating had become a joke. Just for shits and giggles, she opened the app and checked the admirer. The guy lived five hundred miles away, had a blurry picture of himself from twenty years before, and explicitly mentioned in his description that he was "looking for a subservient woman who would take care of all his needs."

She snorted a laugh. *Fuck that noise.* She deleted the request then uninstalled the app from her phone for good. She was done with all that. A small part of her wanted to believe someone was out there for her, but the more she tried, the more everything seemed like wishful thinking. Maybe the universe was playing some sick joke. Aniyah frowned and stared at the mixing bowl. Thoughts about dating were soon forgotten when she realized her more immediate situation. *Rose water.*

Aniyah covered the mixing bowl and set it in the refrigerator. She grabbed her keys and hustled out of her duplex to her car. The heart of Swichester City's rush-hour traffic didn't make things easier as her compact sedan crawled through the streets at a snail's pace. Forty-five minutes later, she finally made it to the main highway and floored the gas pedal. After zooming north toward the suburbs, she veered off the exit ramp and drove toward Cedarstone Heights. With evening fallen, the narrow tree-canopied road was nearly pitch-black, save for the dim light of the full moon. Gripping the steering wheel tightly, Aniyah navigated the winding road. She hated driving it at night. Somehow, she always managed to get lost in that abyss. With not a single streetlight for miles down the road, the turnoff to the general store was easy to miss.

The time was nearing eight o'clock—almost an hour after Ron usually closed shop. Aniyah hoped he would still be there.

Two golden glowing dots suddenly appeared in front of her car, headed straight for her. *Or am I heading for them?* They looked too small to be headlights. *Perhaps bicycle reflectors—*

Holy shit!

She slammed on the brakes. The tires gave an ear-piercing squeal, followed by a loud bang in front of her car. The impact jolted her forward, but the seat belt caught her momentum. Her heart racing, she put the car into park. She took her foot off the brake and let go of the steering wheel. Then she looked around frantically for the bicyclist, but the bike and its rider were nowhere to be found.

"Oh fuck..." she muttered. *Did I just run that bicyclist over? They could be trapped under the car!* She fumbled with the seat belt, grabbed a mini flashlight out of the glove compartment, and scrambled out of the car. She shined the light around the area but saw only a few fallen tree branches. She knelt and checked under the car. Nothing was there, either, not even a bike. *What the hell was that?*

Not wanting to stay a moment longer in such a creepy place, Aniyah returned to her car and buckled her seat belt. As she reached for the handle to close the door, something grabbed her arm. She froze, her fast-beating heart jumping into her throat. She tried to yank her hand away, but pain surged through her wrist as it was squeezed even more tightly. Fear and shock prevented her from screaming. She slowly looked toward the source of the pain to find a shadowy humanlike figure looming over her.

A deep, guttural growl emanated from the stranger.

Aniyah yelped, jumping in her seat, but the seat belt restrained her. She grabbed the flashlight from the passenger's seat and shone it at the stranger. The light revealed thick muscles ridden with tribal tattoos and a brawny shape of a man—a *naked* man. *Oh shit.* As the light touched his face, he threw his arm over his eyes and snarled.

The man's grip around her arm loosened, and Aniyah managed to pull her arm back. She looked at the door again, hoping to close it, but the man was blocking the handle. She grasped the gear selector. She could drive off with the door open if she had to in order to get away from that creep.

As Aniyah was about to put the car in drive, a large figure landed on the hood of her car with a loud bang. She screamed. Two yellow dots glimmered in the darkness, and butterflies filled her stomach. The figure hopped off the hood and disappeared faster than she could blink. What little of the figure's outline she glimpsed looked like a giant dog. *A wolf.*

Her sweaty hand shook on the gear selector as she fumbled to shift into drive. *Wolves! How the hell did I end up in the middle of a wolf pack!*

The mysterious naked man recovered and sneered. "I will rip you apart for that, trespasser!"

Aniyah shivered at his dark, foreboding voice. She strong-armed the gear selector and floored the gas pedal. "I'm not trespassing! This is a public road!" she yelled back at him as the car zoomed off. The driver's-side door flopped open as she roared ahead, unable to reach for the handle to close it. But she would worry about that later once she was away from that angry wolf pack.

She checked her rearview mirror. Dozens of glowing yellow dots were right on her tail. She finally pulled the driver's door shut, her foot never leaving the gas pedal. Looking ahead, she spotted the floodlight affixed to the side of the general store half a mile away, shining down on the wood-chipped parking area in a bluish-white glow.

Aniyah checked her mirror again, and the glowing yellow dots were gone. The wolves must've finally given up and left, unable to keep up with her car. *Good riddance.*

She heaved a deep sigh and returned her attention to the road. Pulling up to the general store, she noticed no cars parked in the lot. A sinking feeling rose in her gut. *Damn it! Is he gone?* she wondered, craning her neck around the corner to see if Ron's car was there. But she found nothing but darkness and shadows behind the building.

Aniyah parked, hopped out of her car, and rushed to the front entrance. To her disappointment, it was dark inside. She swore under her breath. At that point, she didn't give a damn about the rose water anymore. She would just cancel and refund her client's order if she had to. She hated taking the financial hit, especially from a repeat client who paid and tipped more than generously, but a bottle of rose water wasn't worth the cost of barely escaping with her life from rabid shifter clans. The shifter life was vastly different from a human's, and Aniyah, like most humans with common sense, tended to stay out of their complex affairs and mind their own business. But it didn't help that she'd been involuntarily thrown into the middle of a shifter battle. She'd hoped they would be too busy fighting to bother her. *Who knew being a pastry chef could be so dangerous?*

As Aniyah returned to her car, she heard a low, rumbling growl nearby. It sounded different from the wolves' but menacing nonetheless. She swallowed a lump in her throat and looked sidelong toward the source of the sound, which came from somewhere behind the building. But all she saw was shadows.

Fuck this. I'm outta here. She made a beeline for the driver's door. As her sweat-slicked hands reached for the handle, she heard numerous familiar low growls around her. Pulling open the door, she glanced over her shoulder at dozens of glowing yellow dots behind her. Her breathing staggered.

One of the sets of dots emerged from the darkness and approached her. The faint light of the moon outlined the wolf's large shape and reflected the glowing dots of the beast's foreboding eyes. The wolf shifted, its limbs becoming more humanlike, and it stood on two legs instead of four. The mysterious naked man she'd met earlier stood before her.

"I was not done with you, woman," the man growled, then he put a hand on her shoulder and held her in place. "You trespass in our territory, and then you have the audacity to interrupt our ceremonial running by striking one of my sisters with your damned car!"

Aniyah shivered at his icy touch. His grip was firm, and she couldn't shake it off. "It was an accident. I didn't see her," she said, though in the back of her mind, she wondered why the hell she was trying to reason with a naked man who wanted to rip her head off.

She looked around frantically, hoping someone would drive by and help her, but she was way out in the boonies, where nobody would hear her. She was trapped, outnumbered by wolves, cornered like a wounded animal. She was prepared to defend herself as best she could, even if it meant her death—all because she needed rose water.

The man spun her around so that she was facing him. Staring deep into her soul, his human eyes gave off a faint golden glow that made her shiver.

"S-Stay back," Aniyah warned, balling her shaky hands into fists.

One of the other wolves suddenly howled. The man paused, and his eyes locked on something beyond her. He backed away, snarling.

A loud roar and a bang on the car's roof made Aniyah freeze. A shadow loomed over her, breathing heavily. She slowly looked up at the large creature perched on the roof of her car.

A tiger!

The wolf pack seemed to lose interest in Aniyah. Their attention was locked on the tiger, who was poised, ready to strike.

"So, the Whitetide still exists," the naked man said. He returned to all fours and assumed his wolf form once more.

Aniyah watched in confusion, unsure of who was her enemy or ally. She hesitated to get in the car with the giant tiger standing guard, looking like it was going to maul everything in sight, including her.

The snarling wolves stood their ground, the hairs on their backs raised. The tiger assessed the situation, its tail twitching slightly. In a flash, the tiger leapt off the car and landed before the pack. Ignoring the other surrounding wolves, the tiger charged at the bigger wolf. The wolf lunged forward, and they clashed, ending up in a violent tussle on the ground.

The fight blocked Aniyah's only way back to her car. Panicking, she fled and hid behind the wide base of a nearby tree. She cautiously peered around the trunk at the battle. To her relief, the beasts seemed to have lost interest in her.

For several minutes, the wolf and tiger rolled around and fought, mauling and tearing flesh with claws and teeth. Finally, the tiger pinned the wolf beneath its strong body and latched on to the wolf's throat with its jaws. The wolf struggled to get free and let out ear-piercing cries.

The other wolves closed in and pounced on the tiger's back, attempting to take the large animal down in a group effort. But the tiger held firm, tightening its muscles and making his body like an impenetrable shield against the wolves. Still holding the large wolf by the throat, the tiger whipped its head back and forth violently then flung the animal into the trunk of a large tree. The wolf's head smashed against the trunk, and he let out a yelp. His body slid lifelessly to the ground.

Aniyah gawked, wide-eyed. *Holy shit...* She did not want to be next. The way to her car was finally clear. While the tiger was busy squaring off with the remaining pack members, Aniyah made a beeline for her car, hopped into the driver's seat, and started the engine. She checked her rearview mirror and watched as the wolf pack scurried off with their tails between their legs. Two of them retrieved their leader and tugged him along as they followed the rest of their pack back into the woods, where they disappeared.

The tiger was gone—for good, she hoped.

Something suddenly tapped on the passenger-side window. She jumped and looked to her right. A handsome, chiseled—and very naked—Adonis stared back at her with a look of uncertainty in his piercing dark-brown eyes. Through the dimness of the light cast over his olive skin, a certain charm and beauty showed in the man's face. But because looks were deceiving, especially around that area at night, she reeled in her fantasies and regarded the stranger warily. Her stomach clenched as the man's gaze remained fixed on her. He was probably another wolf in disguise.

But then she noticed a string of tiger stripes tattooed down the length of his toned arms. *Not exactly a tattoo that a wolf shifter would have*, she thought.

She continued staring, part of her unable to resist admiring his strong frame, despite it being smeared with dirt and crisscrossed with scratches and bruises.

Wait... is this *guy the tiger?* After what she'd witnessed him do to the large wolf, Aniyah repeatedly hit the lock button to ensure all her doors were secured. She put the car in reverse but kept her foot on the brake as she eyed the man warily.

The stranger looked at her with seemingly genuine concern. "Hey, are you all right?" he asked, his deep voice muffled by the window.

She swallowed. *Is this another shifter trap?* "Who are you? And what do you want?" she yelled back.

The man held up his hands in surrender. "The name's Gauge. Gauge Reed. I was trying to sleep when I heard all the commotion, so I came to help."

Her foot slid off the brake, and the car slowly rolled backward. It wasn't until she saw him following her that she regained herself and quickly slammed her foot back on the brake. She put the car in park. Gauge bumped into the hood of the car and grunted. He shook himself back to his senses and rounded to the driver's side.

He motioned for her to roll down the window. She continued staring at him, willing herself not to let her eyes wander lower. "W-What are you doing out here alone? And naked?" was all she could say.

Gauge plastered his hands and his forehead against the glass, looking at her intently and casting her an amused smile. "I didn't have time to change clothes, so…" He gave a light shrug. "I've been traveling all day. I'm on my way to Greyson Creek and decided to stop and rest for the night."

She half listened to his response and thought about the fact that this handsome hunk had saved her from a certain death. This man actually gave a damn about her. That had to mean something. His voice sounded genuine, and the way he looked at her was the opposite of the sinister gaze the pack leader had given her. Since his concern held some merit, her finger slowly drew to the window switch.

As the window lowered, Gauge pulled back. He gave her a charming smile that outlined a faint scar on his cheek where a dimple would normally be. That smile was contagious, and she couldn't help but return the gesture.

"Thank you," she said.

"No need to thank me. I'm just glad you're safe."

"Yeah, and unfortunately, I wasted a trip out here for nothing."

His brow furrowed. "What do you mean?"

"I have a kitchen emergency and came all the way here, hoping to get some rose water before the store closed. But then I had a run-in with those damned wolves..." She sighed.

His jaw tightened. "They're gone now."

"Will they be back?"

"Hopefully not anytime soon. But you probably shouldn't stick around here for too much longer."

She nodded once. "You don't have to tell me twice. I'm going home. Thank you for saving me from those wolves. I'm Aniyah, by the way."

"Nice to meet you." He nodded absently then paused. "How much is the rose water?"

She furrowed her brow. "Uh, fifteen bucks. Why?"

He patted the driver's-side door reassuringly. "Be back in less than a minute."

Curious, she watched him shift into a large tiger and head toward the store.

CHAPTER 2

As Gauge approached the general store, he thought continuously about that gorgeous, curvaceous woman he'd saved from the wolf attack. *Aniyah...* A beautiful name for a beautiful woman. His tiger was drawn to her like a fated mate. He sensed she had an interesting story, which piqued his feline curiosity. She seemed reserved and cautious—and for good reason, after that harrowing experience with the wolf pack. He hoped a simple good deed like getting her some rose water might earn a little more of her trust.

Gauge shifted back to his human form, grabbed his knapsack from behind the building, and opened it for the first time. He retrieved some clothing—an old pair of jeans, a white, holey T-shirt, a pair of dirty, worn sneakers, and a black baseball cap. They all carried Diesel's scent. *Ugh… really?* Gauge sneered. Cammy had gone and stolen some of Diesel's clothes, risking his wrath. Gauge hoped she knew what she was doing.

Also inside the knapsack were a bag of trail mix, a bottle of water, a razor for shaving, a burner phone, and a hundred bucks. Gauge got dressed, pocketed the money, then walked back to the front of the general store. He stood before the locked doors and pondered the best way to get inside. He could break in, grab a bottle of rose water, and leave the money on the counter. No harm done.

A car door slammed behind him. He glanced over his shoulder.

"Gauge! What are you doing?" Aniyah called, approaching.

He turned back toward the doors. "Getting your rose water. Stay in the car. This won't take long."

She gasped. "No! Don't even think about breaking into that store!"

"But you said it was an emergency. And after all the shit you've had to deal with tonight with those wolves, that can't be all for nothing."

She took a deep breath, and her face softened. "I appreciate your good intentions, but the rose water isn't worth the crime you're about to commit. Please don't do this."

He frowned, noting the hurt in her eyes, the disappointment. "Fine, if that's what you want," he said, drawing back from the door.

"It is. Thanks for your help, anyway. I'm going home now."

Her dismissive tone made the back of his throat tighten. He could potentially lose her forever, never to see her again. She was out of danger—for now—but he still smelled the wolves nearby. Perhaps they were watching and waiting for her to be alone again. Either way, he knew this would not be the last time he encountered them. Wolves were relentless by nature, and they would keep coming back in greater numbers until their alpha was slain. Apparently, the large wolf he'd killed earlier was not the alpha. Gauge figured as much, since that battle felt entirely too easy.

As Gauge was about to respond to Aniyah, the sound of a wolf's howl echoed in the distance. Then another. He glanced around the area with a cautious growl.

Aniyah hugged herself and shuddered. "Oh no... More of them?"

"Their scent is getting stronger. More are coming. C'mon. I'll make sure you get out of here safely."

Her lips formed a thin line with hesitation. Gauge felt her gaze on him as he headed for the passenger's side. "I know we just met," he continued, "but I promise I will try to keep you safe. I am the wolves' target now, not you. But they will not hesitate to kill a human if they get in the way."

"O-Okay... W-Where's your car?"

"Don't have one. I walked a long way. Long story. Eventually, I'll find some transportation. It's been a hell of a week."

Aniyah nodded and climbed into the driver's seat. She started the car and made her way down the dark road. With only the dim moonlight shining above, Aniyah drove slowly. "I hate this road so much," she muttered.

He gave her a reassuring smile. "It is kinda spooky out here, isn't it?"

"Who were those wolves? I've never encountered them before. Then again, I don't normally drive this way at night."

The mention of wolves made him tense up. "They're from the Silverfang Pack, one of my family's many sworn enemies. We have been at war with several wolf clans. The fact that the Silverfangs are out here is not a good sign."

"What do you mean?" Aniyah asked.

"My clan, the Whitetide Streak, currently resides in an area called Greyson Creek, which is about thirty miles north of here. The Silverfang Pack has expanded their territory very close to ours, which means they're most likely up to no good."

"Why would they attack me? I'm not a part of any clan. Hell, I'm not even a shifter!"

He shrugged. "It's what they do. It's a full moon tonight, so they were probably doing their ceremonial running. They can be quite aggressive during that time because some of them are also seeking out mates."

"I see." She stared ahead blankly. "You also killed one of them, so I guess that explains their coming back for revenge."

"That was just the pack leader of their small group, not the clan's alpha." Gauge frowned. Like Axle, he'd claimed victory over the small battles, but the war continued because Xander Silverfang, the alpha, was still alive. *So close and yet so far.*

"Damn…" she muttered under her breath. "All this because of some damn rose water…"

His keen ears perked at her comment. "So, why do you need rose water so badly, anyway?"

"I'm baking a strawberry rosewater cake for a client."

He blinked. "You're a baker?"

"Pastry chef," she corrected, smiling.

"Oh? So that means you're good with your hands, right?"

Her smile turned coy. "You could say that."

"I like a woman who is creative and knows how to build and fix things."

"I build pastries and fix kitchen disasters as they happen." She paused then let out a soft chuckle.

He laughed too. Her sense of humor was refreshing. He couldn't remember the last time a woman had made him smile as much as Aniyah.

They were soon out of the gloom of the canopied road and back on the lighted main road that led to the highway. Aniyah pulled over to the side of the road, under a streetlamp's bright cool-white glow, and put the car in park. The engine still running, she kept her hands gripping the steering wheel and cast a blank stare at the dashboard.

"Thank you again for helping me," she said, not looking at him.

Gauge looked sideways at her. Apparently, his time with her was ending. "No problem..." He slowly put a hand over the door handle. "I hope I can see you again."

Her smile was short-lived. She still kept her eyes averted from him. "Probably not. I'm sure you'll be busy with all your shifter clan business and whatnot... or whatever you guys do."

Damn... so cold... Her ignorance of shifter politics was evident, but that did not deter his tiger from wanting to claim her still. She would pose a challenge, since he was unsure if she would be willing to be a part of shifter society if he claimed her as his mate. The transition was always tough for humans and shifters alike.

"Actually, no," he finally replied. "Not anymore, anyway. But that's a long story." He squeezed the handle. "Well, uh... I guess this is goodbye, then." He slowly got out of the car with a silent hope that she would say something more, but she didn't.

He shut the door and stared at her, sadness and anguish plaguing his inner tiger like a sickness. She still didn't acknowledge him and remained sitting, white-knuckling the steering wheel while she stared blankly at the road ahead. Then she closed her eyes briefly and sighed. Moments later, a smile formed on her lips. She sat back in her seat and released the steering wheel.

Gauge cocked his head to one side. *What is she doing?*

The passenger-side window rolled down halfway. She finally looked at him. "Do you have somewhere to go tonight?" she asked.

"Uh, not really…"

She made a small head gesture, indicating for him to get back in the car.

Gauge stood there, stunned. His tiger, confused and curious, perked up. *Is she serious?* After another bout of hesitation, he slowly reached for the door handle.

"You coming or what?" she asked, her voice tinged with amusement.

Gauge exhaled a breath he'd been holding inadvertently. He flung open the door with glee and plopped back into the passenger's seat. "Did I somehow change your mind?"

Aniyah put the car back in drive and sped off again. "Honestly? I thought chivalry was dead. Especially for someone like me."

Gauge watched her carefully as the glow of passing lights whisked over her face. "What do you mean?"

"Well, for one, never in a million years did I think I'd be rescued from bloodthirsty wolves by a hot, naked tiger-man."

His heart swelled. *She thinks I'm hot? There is hope yet.* "I saw you in trouble and wanted to do the right thing."

"The fact that you would risk your life for a complete stranger is honorable."

"You're a beautiful woman, Aniyah. I would rescue you any day."

She laughed. "That's so cheesy."

"But it's true."

"I'm pretty sure the guys I've been with in the past would've run off scared and left me to fend for myself."

He snorted. "That's what happens when you date human men." *And I'm glad you kicked those guys to the curb.*

When she took the exit ramp leading into Swichester City, Gauge tensed. The city was an hour west of New Rochford. That reminded him of his last encounter with Diesel. The brutal fight had nearly cost Gauge his life, all because of his poor decision to try to get Diesel to fight his battles. But Gauge was spared then, much as he had been during his encounter with Axle. Often, Gauge wondered what else he had to live for if he couldn't even protect himself or fight his own battles. What decent woman would want him as a mate? Though Gauge had tried his hardest in the past to do what he thought was right, his efforts often ended up as complete and utter failures. Tonight, however, was different. He'd followed his instincts and found a potential mate.

Perhaps Aniyah would be his saving grace, a last chance to redeem his honor.

CHAPTER 3

I can't believe I almost just ditched this hot guy after he saved me! Aniyah's fingers ached as she curled and uncurled them from around the steering wheel. Being in Gauge's presence flustered her more than it should've. The fact that he gave a damn about her created some suspicion about what he really wanted with her, if anything. She was afraid to ask, fearing the rejection she'd come to know and accept. Asking too many questions might make him think she was being insecure. But the idea of trusting him left her conflicted. Trust, so easily broken, usually set her up for heartbreak. But perhaps she could at least consider trusting in

Gauge, since he'd saved her life—something no man had ever done for her.

Hell, he'd even been willing to break the law just to get her a bottle of rose water. The whole idea was absurd yet noteworthy. He barely knew her, and he was willing to make sacrifices for her—and risk his own life for her. Gauge carried a spark of chivalry that she hadn't seen in any man she'd met. *It might be nice to get to know him a little more.*

"Are we still in Swichester?" Gauge asked, interrupting her thoughts.

She glanced at him. "Not quite. Just a few miles outside the city limits." She pulled up along the curb in front of a white townhome among the many other identical ones that lined the quiet street. "Here we are. Home sweet home."

Gauge looked ahead. "Cute." He got out of the car.

Aniyah followed suit and made her way to the front stoop of her unit.

Gauge stopped short of the stoop and stared up at her, smiling. The ominous scar on his cheek returned.

Aniyah admired the rest of his physique. He was even bigger up close. The rigid muscles in his arms were defined, as if he'd done hard labor all his life.

She shifted her thoughts and rummaged in her purse for her house key. Part of her hoped he'd want to stay over for a little while. She didn't have anything else left to do that night. Without rose water, she was out of a contract, and the rest of the night would be pretty lonely and boring. Besides, she would love to get to know her handsome savior a bit more. "Would you, um… like to stay for a while?" she offered, her cheeks getting hot. "Unless you've got stuff to do tonight."

Gauge's eyes widened a moment, and he beamed. "I could think of nothing better than to spend an evening with a gorgeous woman like you."

Her heart fluttered. *He thinks I'm gorgeous.* She'd never heard a man utter that word about her—and actually mean it, anyway. His sincerity made her more curious about him.

"Okay." She opened the front door and walked inside. She flipped on the living-room light as Gauge shut the door behind himself.

"I like this setup," he said, looking around. "Small, quiet, and cozy."

"Thank you." She headed to the kitchen. Gauge had made more meaningful compliments to her in one night than all the other men she'd been with combined. "Want something to drink?" she called, opening the fridge. She stared blankly at the bowl of cake batter she would soon have to find another use for.

"No, thanks." His voice was so close to her that she froze.

She hadn't heard him follow her. *Figures. A tiger-man like him would be extra stealthy.* She shut the fridge, retrieved a bottle of rum from the liquor cabinet, and poured herself a glass. Heaven knew she needed it. "Okay, then."

"So this is where you make magic, eh?" Gauge said, admiring her tiny kitchen.

She laughed. "What magic? All I need is a stove, an oven, and a fridge, and I'm golden." She took a gulp of her drink.

"So, uh… What about your rose water cake?" Gauge asked.

That damn cake. "It's too late to call my client about it now. I'll have to call her first thing in the morning and cancel the order. There's no way I'll have it finished by ten a.m. tomorrow for their special event." She sighed. "Six hundred dollars down the drain."

He blinked. "Six hundred dollars for a cake?"

"It's a specially decorated gourmet cake for one of my top clients."

"Is that why you drove such a long way just to get some rose water?"

"Yes. That store is the only place around that sells the Niagua brand I use. Besides, I know the owner, and he usually cuts me a break on the price."

"I see." Gauge rubbed the light-brown scruff on his chin.

She took another gulp and made her way back to the living room. "So... I wanna know the man behind the tiger. And why someone like you would give a damn about someone like me."

He followed her as she brushed past and plopped down next to her on the couch. "The man behind the tiger? That's a complicated question. I've been away from home for many months, traveling around and trying to figure out who I am and what my purpose is. I'm a man of many failures and bad decisions. It's caused a rift between me and my family. But as I see the world from a different perspective, I'm trying to learn how to fix my mistakes and find my purpose again."

She tilted her head. "That sounds so... poetic. You are a man of mystery."

"I like to think I am."

"Do you work?"

"Not currently. It's complicated."

She wrinkled her nose slightly. Yet another guy without a car, job, or anything else going for him. She seemed to be a magnet for the deadbeats and odd ones who had no idea what to do with their lives. But no man had ever risked his life for her like Gauge had, which kept alive a hope that maybe beneath his ragged exterior, he was really a good guy.

"Ehh..." She shrugged. "Shifters in general are complicated. I don't understand the weird shit you all do."

He chuckled. "It's how our kind survives. Getting caught up in shifter affairs can seem daunting, but..." He paused and stared at her intently. "A shifter's number-one priority is to protect their mate."

She met his gaze and nodded, slowly and thoughtfully. She sensed he was talking to her soul as he said those words. *"Protect their mate..." Is that his way of saying he's into me?* A small lump formed in the back of her throat. It couldn't have been true. A handsome man like Gauge probably already had a beautiful bombshell of a mate. All the handsome, caring guys were always taken. Besides, Aniyah didn't exactly see herself as a man's preferred type. She was an independent, thick, apple-shaped girl who ran a successful business on her own. Some men who had nothing to bring to the table tended to be intimidated by that fact. Gauge, however, seemed to challenge it.

"I'm sure your mate will be very happy to know that you saved a life tonight," she said wistfully then took a long sip of her rum.

He raised his eyebrows. "I don't have a mate."

She nearly choked on her rum. "You're joking, right? You can't possibly be single."

His head cocked to the side. "Why is that so hard to imagine?"

"Why? Well… I mean… look at you. You're fucking hot. You're kind, chivalrous, and you save damsels in distress. There's no other way to say it. What woman wouldn't want to snag you up in a heartbeat?"

"Oh…" His smile broadened. "Is that what you think about me?"

Her cheeks burned. *Does he really not have a mate, or is he just playing games?* "It's what I know. Men like you don't want thick girls. And they sure as hell don't want an independent woman who's got her shit together. All they want is someone who will"—she sneered—"tend to their needs…"

He blinked several times then burst out laughing. "Are you fucking kidding me? I don't know what men you've been hanging around, but they all sound like a bunch of stupid motherfuckers who probably don't even know which hole to put it in."

She gawked at his response then suddenly laughed, too, realizing the absurdity of her own statement.

"There. I made you laugh. I bet none of those other dickheads ever did that." His smile turned coy.

"No, they didn't," she said, thinking back on her numerous failed relationships and dating disasters. They didn't so much as give her a compliment.

"So, as you can see, I'm not like other men. I adore a thick girl who's independent and loves working with her hands. A shifter's mate is strong and independent in their own right. And I'm not afraid to say that I'm attracted to you, even if we've only just met by fate."

The sincerity in his tone made her heart swell with adoration. Apparently, he was for real. *Is this really happening to me right now?* No, Gauge was not like other men. He was not only different—he was mysterious. And he wasn't afraid to admit his flaws.

He was as real as real could get. Yet hesitation still plagued her mind. She'd been hurt too many times and didn't want to go through the process all over again. "You have a way with words. But as you said, we've only just met, and I don't know if I'm ready to jump into another relationship right now."

"I understand and respect that. It's refreshing to see a woman like you take charge of her own life."

She chewed on her bottom lip as she considered her next question. His response could go either way, depending on how he would interpret it. "Uh… Do you need a place to stay for the night? I don't have much room, but you can sleep on the couch if you want…"

His smile grew. "As tempting as it is, I'm going to have to take you up on that offer another time. Nothing to do with you, by the way. There are some things I need to deal with alone. I'll find a motel in town or something to stay at in the meantime. But I appreciate the offer."

She exhaled slowly, her mind flooding with thoughts. He'd refused but not for the reason she'd assumed. He seemed to have some personal issues going on, and she respected that. Still, it gave her hope that Gauge might really be the breath of fresh air that she needed in her life. "So… um…" She fished for another subject. "Do you do anything for fun? Any hobbies?"

"Eh… I like tinkering with machines. Cars, mainly," Gauge replied.

"Oh! Are you a car mechanic?… Wait. Your name. It makes sense now. Is Gauge really your name?"

He snorted. "Unfortunately, yeah. Believe me, my siblings and I have heard every joke in the book."

"What joke?"

He rolled his eyes. "When your gearhead father names his kids Axle, Gauge, Diesel, and Cammy, you tend to become the butt of every car joke known to man."

She blinked. *He has siblings? I can't imagine anyone more charming than him.* "Well, you don't have to worry about that with me. I'm not enough of a car enthusiast to find humor in such things."

"Damn. Your hotness level just went up even further."

She hid her smile, amused by his cheesy line. "Why? Because I'm not a car enthusiast?"

"No, because you just don't give a fuck."

She laughed. The way he said it so innocently, like he was new to picking up women, emphasized his unique tenderness and charm. "You're too much."

"I've wanted to meet someone for a long time. But so many things have been going on in my life that I've never had the opportunity. Maybe our meeting could be the start of something special— hopefully long-term."

Am I dreaming? A guy that actually wants a long-term relationship? "Wait. Did I hear that correctly?"

His brow furrowed. "What?"

"The guys I've met in the past were always just looking for quick booty calls. You totally threw me off when you said were looking for something long-term."

"Many shifters mate for life. I don't want a quick booty call. I want a family."

Her mouth opened slightly. He'd echoed her own desires. Maybe their fateful meeting wasn't an accident. *So this is Gauge Reed: caring, sweet, attentive, eager, and as hot as fuck.* She gave him a crafty grin. "Too bad you're not a chef, too, or else we could both make magic in the kitchen."

He mirrored her expression. "Hey, I fix cars, not plates. But I can make a mean grilled-cheese sandwich."

She laughed. *Add a sense of humor to his list of desirable traits.* Aniyah thought she could learn to like this tiger-man.

CHAPTER 4

*F*UCK! *I CAN'T BELIEVE I turned down her offer to stay
with her!*

The thought repeated in his mind as he grabbed
his bag and saw himself out the door of Aniyah's
house. He'd finally left at one o'clock in the
morning, after the two of them spent time talking
and getting to know each other. That night, his
rational side defeated his lust. His tiger understood
that it was not yet time to claim her when he first
needed to earn her full trust. She was probably still
rattled from her encounter with the Silverfang Pack.
He had so much to tell her, but he also didn't want
to bog her down with clan politics. However, he also
wasn't making himself sound very appealing when

it didn't seem like he had much going for him. His journey of self-discovery had taken an awkward turn. But he was determined to find the right path to victory. He wanted to see her smile again, and he had an idea how. He just hoped he was making the right choice.

Gauge trekked the three miles back to Swichester City. He remained in his human form so as not to attract attention. As he walked, he scanned the area for the nearest motel. He would stay there a while to plan his next move. The earlier encounter with Silverfang wolves was no accident, since they were one of the Whitetide Streak's most formidable enemies. If Gauge could find and kill Xander, that would be a huge victory for his clan. Defeating such a powerful enemy might make Axle yield to Gauge without any bloodshed, but Gauge wasn't betting on it. Being cut from the same cloth, Axle was as stubborn as he was. Gauge knew finding the Silverfang alpha wasn't going to be easy, and going to look alone would've been a death sentence.

The buzzing neon sign of a shabby motel on the side of the road came into view just before the bridge leading into the city. A couple of junk cars were parked out front among other mounds of trash and scrap metal. Gauge approached the office door and spotted a half-decent motorcycle leaning against the wall beneath a humming, dim dome light. Some of the chrome was rusted, as though it had been a victim of the harsh elements. The thing looked like it hadn't been ridden in a long time, judging by the dust and dirt on the leather seat. Gauge loved motorcycles, and he'd regretted selling his own months before, when he left New Rochford.

He jiggled the handle to the office's front door, and to his surprise, it was open. The closet-sized office stank of mildew and spoiled food. A small wooden desk sat in the midst of trash and debris. Sitting at the edge of the desk was a tiny silver bell with a taped label on it that read Ring Bell for Service.

Gauge wrinkled his nose. He'd stayed in worse places. And living off the land was as brutal as it got. He approached the desk and tapped his finger on the bell. Moments later, a skinny mature woman appeared from another room beyond the desk. Her short blond hair bore the faint dark patterns of cheetah spots.

"Hey there. Just you tonight?" the woman asked, retrieving a thick book from beneath a pile of loose papers.

"Yep. Name's Gauge Reed. Just staying for a night. Maybe two."

She scanned him up and down with her gaze. "*Maybe?* Yeah, okay." Smirking, she opened the book to a dog-eared page and scribbled his name onto one of the blank spaces.

"You own this place?"

"Sure do. The name's Lucille. It's twenty bucks a night, by the way."

Twenty bucks for this dump? "Fine, whatever." He forked over the money. "Whose bike is that, out front?"

She stopped writing and looked up at him curiously. "That old jalopy? I think it belonged to some rough biker-looking guy who stayed here last year. He owed me two nights' pay. I went to collect but found out he was gone and left his bike behind. Ain't never seen him since."

Gauge blinked. "He just vanished?"

"Seemed that way. I think he got himself killed, if you ask me. He was running with a rough crowd. I'm still pissed he stiffed me forty bucks, though."

"Does the bike still work?"

"Nah, that piece of junk ain't worked since the guy left. I would've gotten rid of it by now, but I kept hoping that maybe he'd eventually come back for it. Then I can get my forty bucks."

He snorted. "If he's dead, I don't think he'll be coming back."

"Yeah, you're probably right... It bugs the hell out of me."

He rubbed his chin. "How much do you want for it? I'll take it off your hands."

She flashed a grin. "Forty bucks."

"For fuck's sake... Fine. Whatever. Deal. I can probably get it working again."

"You some kinda mechanic or something?"

"I tinker with cars here and there." He shrugged.

Her face lit up. "Really? Okay. How's this: I got a car out back that needs fixing. Damn thing won't start worth a shit. If you get it working, too, then you can stay here for free."

"Oh, wow. What a deal. It's the same price I'd be paying to stay here."

"Hey, I'm running a business here. Take it or leave it."

He considered her offer. Getting roped into a possibly complicated car project was something unexpected. Perhaps that was one thing he had to thank his gearhead father for. Gauge was the only one of his siblings who'd actually shown an interest in cars, and his father dumped all that knowledge into him. As a result, Gauge was adept at fixing practically anything that had an engine. "Eh… okay. I'll do it, but if it turns out I need parts for the car, then that cost is on you."

Lucille wrinkled her nose slightly then scratched one side of her jaw in thought. "Ugh… fine. Whatever it takes to fix it. I've called every damn towing company in town, and each one has some lame excuse or another as to why they can't come out here."

"Damn. It's not like you live that far from the city…"

"Right? I haven't been able to go nowhere for two days. Anyway…" She took out a set of keys from the desk drawer then plucked a single bronze key from a wooden pegboard behind the desk and handed them to him. "This one's your room key— room number nine. And these are the car keys. The black one out back."

"Got it." He swiped the keys, plunked down the forty bucks for the bike, then turned and walked out the door. On his way to his room, he wheeled the motorcycle along. Surprisingly, despite having been abandoned for so long, the tires still looked good. He leaned the motorcycle against the wall outside his door then entered his room. The miniature room's run-down condition rivaled that of the motel's exterior, with its stained walls and ceilings, grungy carpet, and shabby wooden furniture. The decades-old television sitting on a rickety stand looked like it'd seen better days and was probably just there more for decoration than an actual working appliance. But at least the room had a bed, toilet, tub, and sink—all that Gauge needed for his short stay.

He retreated to the bathroom and took a nice hot shower. Getting the smell of the woods off himself was a relief. Afterward, he stepped out of the shower, refreshed, brushed his teeth with the new toothbrush he'd picked up from the general store, and fished in his bag for the razor. He smiled to himself, thinking of Cammy in that moment and how thoughtful she was to remember to pack the little things for him. He grimaced at his reflection in the water-spotted mirror. He hadn't shaved in almost a month and was starting to look like his old friend Barron Austin. Gauge missed the big bear, who had been by his side as they ran an auto business together for a short while in New

Rochford. Barron was a member of the Blacktail Clan, a clan of black bears, who, for a time, were long-standing allies of the Whitetide Streak. During Axle's rule, however, that alliance had been severed. But that hadn't affected Gauge and Barron's friendship. Gauge decided it was about time he returned to New Rochford at some point to see him. Perhaps with the Silverfang Wolves posing a threat, it might behoove Gauge to call upon his friend for help.

The little sleep he'd gotten back at Cedarstone Heights was enough to keep him going a little while longer, at least until his body completely rebelled. He had unfinished business at that backwater town, unfinished business with Aniyah. But first, he needed to deal with his transportation. He went back outside and examined the motorcycle. The key was still in the ignition, a skull key ring hanging from it. Trying his luck, he cranked the engine. Nothing happened. He found the bike's tool kit in one of its hidden compartments and got to work. That morning was going to be a long one.

An hour later, Gauge located the root of the problem: a rusted fuel control valve. Gauge could probably rebuild it or rig one up if he had to. He'd learned quite a few tricks from his crafty father, who could build practically anything from scrap parts. During his inspection, he'd also noticed the bike still had oil, and the tank contained a bit of fuel, but one sniff told him it would need to be replaced.

He left the bike and scoured the motel's junky premises for spare parts. After two in the morning, the night was pitch black, but his tiger's darkvision allowed him to see things clearly. He collected the parts he needed and wandered to the back of the motel, where a lone black car was parked. Unlike the others out front, this car looked fairly modern, cleaned up, and drivable. It must've belonged to Lucille. He got into the driver's seat and turned the key in the ignition. The console lit up, but the engine made no sound, not even a click.

Well, it's not the battery, at least. Sure hope it's nothing too complicated, he thought then popped the hood. His tiger's darkvision revealed every detail of the car's inner workings without the use of a flashlight. After several minutes of fiddling around with wires, belts, and connectors, Gauge pinpointed the problem—a faulty ignition coil. He pulled out the coil, which was cracked and warped, as though it had been set on fire. *Yep, that would do it.* Replacing it would be easy, but getting a new coil would have to wait until later that morning, when the auto shops opened. And he sure as hell didn't feel like building one from scratch. He located the car's highway kit in the trunk and found a portable battery charger—just what he needed.

Gauge returned to the motorcycle and got to work rebuilding the petcock. His hands worked autonomously, and he became lost in his own world, letting his thoughts wander, namely to Aniyah. He'd only just met her, but she intrigued his tiger. She was an independent woman who had her shit together, one of many strengths he admired in a mate. He wasn't sure about her battle skills, but he sensed a strong fire in her that she wouldn't hesitate to unleash if someone pissed her off far enough. *A strong woman, a strong mate,* his father would often say about his mother. His parents died together in battle—in love.

Two hours passed, and Gauge had rebuilt and reinstalled the petcock. Afterward, he walked to the nearest twenty-four-hour service station to fill up a fuel canister then returned to the motel. He hooked the bike up to the portable battery charger and prayed that the battery didn't have a dead cell. While it was charging, he rigged up a siphon out of some old junk and drained the old fuel from the tank into an empty steel drum. Afterward, he did his best to clean up the rest of the body with an old scrap of cloth. As he wiped away the grime and dirt, he stared at his reflection in the chrome. His eyes gave off a subtle golden glow, which indicated his activated darkvision.

The old fuel removed, he poured in the new fuel. The battery on the charger read fifteen percent—still a ways to go but enough to test out the bike. He turned the key in the ignition. The dash panel atop the gas tank lit up. He turned the key farther, flipped the ignition switch, and started the engine. It turned and turned, straining to catch.

"C'mon, baby, you got this," he muttered under his breath.

Moments later, the engine caught, and he breathed a sigh of relief. He revved the engine a few times, the odor of burned debris and dust from the pipes assaulting his nose. He let the engine idle for a bit before giving it some more juice. With a sigh of relief, he returned to his room. He grabbed a pen and notepad from the night table and scribbled a note to Lucille, letting her know that he'd found the problem with her car and would be back later with the new part. After he finished, he folded the note, walked it down to the main office, and slid it under the door. He returned to the motorcycle, which was still running well on its own. The battery was charged up to only twenty-five percent, but that was enough to get him going. He packed up the charger and tool kit in his knapsack, slipped it on over his back, and mounted the bike. He left the motel parking lot and zipped down the street. To his relief, it still rode well. The time had come to put his plans into motion.

In an uneventful forty-five minutes, he zipped back up to Cedarstone Heights and parked in front of the general store. He plugged the charger into an unused outlet outside the store and hooked it up to the motorcycle's battery. Then he settled onto the ground and leaned against the parked bike. He gazed up at the sky, and judging by the location of the rising moon, Gauge figured the time was around five in the morning. With that thought, he closed his eyes and decided to catch a quick nap.

A distant wolf's howl suddenly jolted him awake. The sky was still dark, and only minutes seemed to have passed since he closed his eyes. Gauge sniffed and detected the scent of wolf in the air, so he shrugged out of his clothes and shifted into his tiger form. He let out a mighty roar, announcing his presence and daring any Silverfang wolf to challenge him.

"Come at me, you motherfuckers!" he projected to any nearby wolf who could hear him.

Two sets of glowing yellow eyes appeared from the pitch blackness of the trees. Then two wolves emerged. They were smaller in stature and weaker, and Gauge presumed they were patrols. They would be an easy defeat for Gauge, so he decided to let them take the first swing if they dared.

"Who's first?" Gauge projected.

The wolves exchanged glances with each other then lowered their bodies to the ground.

Gauge could sense their trepidation. His height and strength dwarfed their own.

"You're a fool to come back here," one of the wolves replied.

"My business here is not with you… yet."

The other wolf snarled. *"Xander will deal with you soon enough. Once he's taken care of that damned human woman who hurt our dearest sister."*

He perked up. *"If you dare touch her…"*

The wolves howled in unison. *"The Silverfangs will rise! You tigers are as good as dead!"* Then they turned and ran back into the woods.

Gauge was tempted to follow but decided against it as he sensed a death trap. He knew he couldn't take on the entire Silverfang Pack—

including the alpha—alone. *Cowards,* he thought, letting out a frustrated growl. Then he assumed his human form once more, got dressed, and returned to his spot next to his motorcycle. He wouldn't leave that place—he couldn't—until his task was complete. And that wouldn't happen for another few hours. He shut his eyes once more. As he slept, his tiger's keen senses of hearing and smell remained alert for the slightest hint of wolf.

"Hey, you."

Gauge opened his eyes and stared up at a man looming over him. The sky was no longer dark, and he'd lost track of time. The early-morning light cast shadows around him, enhancing the stranger's ominous presence. Gauge's eyes finally adjusted to the light, and he tensed. His tiger was on edge after being disturbed from his rest. He sniffed once and relaxed. The man did not carry the scent of wolf.

"No loitering 'round my store," the stranger continued, scowling.

Gauge yawned and straightened. "I was waiting for it to open up."

The man's gaze steeled. "You slept out here all night just to wait for the store to open?"

"Yep. I need some rose water ASAP."

A slight crinkle appeared in the man's brow. "Rose water?"

"Yeah. Niagua brand. For a friend."

"This 'friend' doesn't have the name Aniyah, do they?"

Gauge raised his eyebrows. "How did you know?"

"She's the only customer who buys Niagua-brand rose water from this store." The man approached the front door and unlocked it. "A friend of Aniyah is okay by me. I'm Ron, by the way."

"Gauge." He hopped to his feet and followed Ron inside.

Aniyah awoke to her cell phone's insistent buzzing. Groaning, she rolled over and grabbed it. She caught a glimpse of Ron's number, along with the time: 8:25 a.m.

"Hello?" she answered groggily.

"Mornin,' Ms. Aniyah. Wanted to let you know I got your rose water delivered."

Aniyah sat up in bed. "What?"

"I'm just passin' along a message. Can't wait to taste your banana nut bread!"

She opened her mouth to speak, but the line went dead. *What did he mean by that?*

Her doorbell suddenly rang. She started then hopped out of bed. She grabbed her robe from the closet, slipped it on, and hurried to the front door. The mysterious visitor was gone. A wine bag with a note attached sat on her doorstep.

She widened her eyes. *Rose water?* She'd been ready to call her client about canceling the job. *How'd this get here?* She brought the bag inside and unfolded the note.

Rose water for the most beautiful rose I've met.

—Gauge

She gasped, shocked that he'd gone all the way back to Cedarstone Heights for her. She unpacked the rose water. Niagua—the exact brand she needed. Gauge had remembered. She grinned. She wouldn't have to cancel after all. And if she got started on the fondant right away, she would be able to get the cake finished and delivered before the event in two hours. Her heart pounded furiously. It was such a stupid, petty thing, yet Gauge cared enough about her to go through all that trouble. He *was* serious, and any doubts she'd had about him before were gone. She wanted to call Gauge and thank him, but she realized that after all that time she'd spent with him the night before, she never got his number. Her mind was rattled by being so caught up in him, and she was still flustered after the previous night's events. She called Ron instead. Maybe Gauge would stop at the store again soon.

"Mornin' again, Ms. Aniyah," Ron drawled.

"Ron, I got Gauge's package. I wanted to tell him thanks, but I don't know how to reach him. If you see him again, will you tell him for me? And give him my number?"

Ron chuckled. "Now, Ms. Aniyah, I think you should be tellin' him yourself."

"But I don't know when I'll see him again."

"Oh, he seems like the travelin' type. I'm sure you'll see him again soon. Now, if that's all, I'll leave you to your love connection. I've got work to do."

She snorted. "Love connection?"

"Why not? He looks like a fine young man for a pretty lady like you."

She blushed. *Yeah, he sure is fine.* "Thank you, but we've only just met. There's nothing going on between us."

There was a brief pause. "Have a nice day, Ms. Aniyah," he said with an obvious smile in his voice then ended the call.

CHAPTER 5

Gauge stared at New Rochford's approaching skyline as he sped along the main highway. He hadn't set foot in the city in six months. Since the night Diesel had nearly killed him, Gauge had stayed away from his brother's territory, not wanting to tempt fate. Diesel was a man of his word, and Gauge knew his brother wouldn't hesitate to kill him if they met again.

But after meeting and spending time with Aniyah the night before, Gauge had been evaluating his own life, his purpose, his reason for being. He couldn't sit around and let the embarrassment of his failures continue, though. He seemed to be the only one who gave a shit about preserving his family's honor, and he vowed to do what he could to make things right… even if that meant tempting fate again.

With Aniyah having entered his life, Gauge knew he couldn't fail again. More than ever, he wanted to take over the Whitetide Streak and claim Aniyah as his mate. With her ruling at his side, he would have a new purpose, to continue the family line, and would rebuild and restrengthen the ties to the clan's allies that Axle had had severed. Their bond would restore the Whitetide Streak to its strength and former glory.

He sensed Aniyah's pain. People she had cared for had disappointed her, and Gauge was not about to be the next one. He would do everything in his power to gain and keep her love and trust.

There was no task too small he wouldn't do for her—even something as trivial as getting her some rose water, an ordeal that endangered her life just because she was in the wrong place at the wrong time. Gauge had delivered it to her doorstep, where she would be sure to see it. He would give her the space she needed to do what she loved doing, and he would support her in every way. And when the time was right, he would claim her.

Gauge pulled up in front of his old auto shop. The building looked like it had a fresh coat of paint, and the new shingle hanging out front read Barron's Auto Body. Dozens of cars were parked outside, waiting to be serviced.

Gauge smiled. *Great to see business is still booming.* He snapped down the kickstand and dismounted his motorcycle. Standing before the auto shop, he felt his body suddenly tense. He was not far from Diesel's gym. Though unable to detect his brother's scent in the air, Gauge remained on edge.

He adjusted his backward baseball cap and strode toward one of the shop's open bays, where a car was up on a lift. Gauge's best friend, Barron Austin, was underneath, tinkering with the muffler. Two other guys were working on a pickup in the adjacent bay. One guy had his head under the hood, while the other sat in the driver's seat, examining a machine monitor.

Glad he has hired help, Gauge thought. Before Gauge left, it had been just the two of them.

Gauge leaned against the steel frame of the bay and whistled to Barron.

The big, burly man stopped tinkering and looked toward him with narrowed eyes. Once

Barron recognized Gauge, his gruff, dark-bearded face lit up. "Holy shit! Is that you, Gauge?"

Gauge nodded and pushed off the frame. The two of them met halfway and did their secret handshake, followed by a shoulder bump. Gauge looked Barron up and down. He was still the same six-foot-five giant bear of a man Gauge remembered. "How've you been?"

Barron grinned and gestured toward the shop. "Great. Steady business, hardworking employees, happy customers. We got a great thing going here."

Gauge smiled and nodded. "That's great, man. I knew I left this place in good hands."

Barron returned the smile then slapped Gauge's back. "Damn, where've you been all this time? It seems like it's been forever."

Gauge's smile fell, and he looked around a moment. "Only about six months, but yeah. I've been around. Some things have happened in those months." He looked at Barron carefully and lowered his voice. "I need to talk to you."

Barron nodded curtly and gestured toward the office.

Gauge followed him into the office and shut the door behind himself. He leaned back against the door and sighed.

Barron faced him, crossing his arms. "What's up?"

"I'm in deep shit, man. I can use your help."

"Uh-oh. What'd you do this time?"

"I didn't do anything. It's my fucking brother, Axle. He's gone and turned practically every clan around us into enemies."

Barron scowled, walked over to the desk, and plopped down in the chair. He leaned back, and the chair gave a familiar squeak. Once upon a time, Gauge had sat in that same chair, at the same desk. "Yeah, I heard through the grapevine some shitstorm's starting with you Whitetides."

"When is it not? Anyway, it's not me. It's Axle. He's determined to fuck up our name with his bullshit leadership. I tried to get Diesel to fight him. At least he has his head on straight to be a better leader than Axle could ever be. But as much as I tried to piss him off enough to get him riled up to fight Axle, he refused. Anyway, I took the worst of that backfired plan." Gauge ran his hand along the faint scar on his cheek, where Diesel had struck him.

Barron made a face. "Shit, man. Well, why don't you confront Axle again?"

"I intend to but not yet." He combed his fingers through his hair. "I need your help with something else, though."

"Name it."

"I ran into some Silverfang wolves last night." Gauge recounted the incident at Cedarstone Heights.

Barron heaved a huge sigh and rubbed his temples as though finding the story difficult to process. "Wow, what a shitty night. Of all the wolf packs, you just *had* to get caught up with the Silverfang. My clan had a close run-in with those fuckers a long time ago."

"Thanks to Axle, there's a target on the Whitetide Streak. I want to take out the Silverfang's leader, Xander. With him gone, it would send a message to the other rival clans who dare mess with the Whitetide Streak."

Barron paused. "But if you die in the process, it'll only exacerbate the problem."

Gauge cringed. "I understand the risks. But I have to try because nobody else will. Besides all that, they threatened the life of someone I care about."

Barron raised his eyebrows. "Your mate?"

"She's not my mate… yet. But soon, I hope."

"No offense, man, but your clan will be obliterated in minutes if you guys try to take on the Silverfang Pack yourselves. They have large numbers."

Gauge shook his head. "Who said anything about my clan helping? Axle is too much of a coward to ever allow it. I'm going to have to go at this alone, with the help of allies."

Barron looked thoughtful for a moment. "I'll talk to my family."

"Oh, man, if the Blacktail Clan can help me, then we can easily take out the Silverfang."

"Yeah, but given the current leadership of your clan, I doubt many will want to join the cause."

"Can't you tell them that I'm not with Axle anymore?" Gauge shrugged.

"Don't matter. You're still a Whitetide tiger." Barron hardened his gaze. "Even if my family does agree, it's going to be a tough battle. The Silverfangs are fearless."

Gauge lifted his head. "So am I. The alpha is mine. I'm willing to fight to my death if it means there's a chance my family's honor will be spared." His heart pounded furiously, and his body tensed with fear—not fear of dying but fear of failing yet again.

CHAPTER 6

ANIYAH COULDN'T BELIEVE HOW WELL the cake turned out, and she was able to hand deliver it just in time for her client's business leaders' event. The client, Mary Stranton, was one of the most respected business leaders in the city, and she couldn't stop gushing over the baroque-decorated, double-layer cake topped with a small three-dimensional rose water fondant replica of her company's red stallion logo.

"I'm glad you like it," Aniyah said into the phone with a smile.

"Like it? Seriously, Aniyah, you've outdone yourself. You really need to stop working at home and open up your own sweet shop."

Though that was Aniyah's dream, she wasn't sure if she was ready to take that leap of faith yet. "I've thought about it."

"Make it happen. I'll even find you some investors. This *needs* to happen. We don't have a good sweet shop around here."

Aniyah gave a hollow laugh.

"Anyway, I just had to call to tell you that. I'm going to be spreading the word about you at this business leaders' event, so I'm sure you'll be getting some inquiries soon."

"Thank you." Aniyah beamed. With Mary so heavily involved, Aniyah was sure to get a lot of business. *All because of Gauge's selfless act of getting me that damned rose water!*

After ending the call, Aniyah sprawled out on her bed and stared up at the ceiling. Gauge had so much faith in her that he'd gone out of his way to help her. Her heart swelled with excitement. She couldn't wait to tell him the good news about the cake. Maybe she could see him again too. She cursed herself again for forgetting to ask for his number.

Aniyah hopped out of bed and headed to the kitchen. All that work had riled her appetite. She was preparing a ham sandwich when her doorbell rang.

She crept to the door and peered out the peephole. Her silent prayers were answered when she saw the fish-eye image of Gauge's dangerously handsome face looking back.

Aniyah blushed. Her heart felt like it was going to leap out of her chest. With a bright smile, she flung open the door. "Gauge! I was just thinking about you!"

Gauge beamed. "Well, damn, looks like I came just in time, then."

She let him in and gushed about the news.

When she'd finished, Gauge said, "I don't see how anyone would *not* enjoy anything you make."

"I've been encouraged to expand my business beyond my home and get an actual establishment—a bakery," Aniyah said. "I've been on the fence about it. My poor oven is going to die once I get another influx of new orders, thanks to the word of mouth of my number one client."

"I think it's a great idea. You should do it."

She sighed. "But I can only imagine the amount of paperwork involved in opening a bakery."

Gauge nodded. "I can help you with that. After all, I opened my own auto shop."

She clasped and unclasped her hands, still feeling doubtful. Then she suddenly felt him draw closer, close enough that she could feel the heat from his body. He smelled like a garage—oil, gasoline, metal, and a little sweat.

She looked up at him and blushed. "Did you just come from work?"

He flashed a crooked smile. "Not exactly. I had to finish repairing someone's car before I came here. And I fixed up my motorcycle a bit more too."

"You have a motorcycle?" She blinked.

"I do now. It's my new baby. I'll have to take you for a ride sometime."

His response drew a small smile out of her. Gauge was such a selfless man, seemingly helping everyone he could. Maybe he had more going for him than she'd originally thought.

"As for you..." he continued, putting his hand on her shoulder. "Stop stressing about that bakery. You don't have to decide now."

Aniyah froze, his reassuring touch sending hot sparks through her body. She opened her mouth to respond, but no sound came out. Flustered, she averted her gaze.

Gauge drew his hand to her chin, gently tilting it toward him, urging her to look at him.

She gazed into his rich brown eyes and swallowed. He stared deep into her soul, awakening a desire she hadn't felt in so long.

"But if it means I get to see your beautiful smile again," he continued in a low tone, "I'll find you the perfect place in no time."

His deep voice sent a shiver down her spine. Rivets of goose bumps tickled her forearms. Her cheeks burned. "Ah… y-you don't have to do that."

"I want to. And I will if you'll let me."

His insistence made her smile. "I'll deal with it when the time comes."

He sighed and dropped his hand from her face. Already missing his touch, she could see the slight dejection in his eyes. That wasn't how she wanted things to end up.

She took his hand. "Why don't you join me for lunch?"

Gauge had learned early on to never reject anything Aniyah offered, especially when it came to her hospitality. He leaned against the doorframe of the kitchen, his arms crossed, and watched the sexy pastry chef construct two ham sandwiches. Even for such a simple dish, Aniyah was meticulous in making the sandwiches, even cutting them into perfect equal halves.

His eyes flicked down to the white apron tied around her curvy waist and plump belly, secured by a little bow that sat perfectly on her nice round ass. His mind wandered and fantasized about the sexy things he would do to her if she made more of her exceptional pastries while wearing that same apron and nothing underneath.

"You're not gonna put whipped cream and sprinkles on them, are you?" Gauge joked.

Aniyah gave him a puzzled look. "Eww… Why would I do that to a ham sandwich?"

Gauge shrugged, giving her an amused look. "Well, what else would I expect from a pastry chef?"

She laughed. "If you want a sweet dessert, I can create you something."

He exhaled slowly at her offer. *Oh, I want dessert, all right.* "I'm not really a sweets guy, but I'll try it if you make it."

It was just his luck that he would hook up with a pastry chef when he lacked the ability to taste sweet things, a curse of his feline shifter kind. He regretted that he would never be able to enjoy any of Aniyah's homemade desserts.

"All right, no sweets for you. I'll keep that in mind." She handed him a plate. "Here's your unsweetened ham sandwich."

The sandwich was garnished with a cherry tomato cut into four slices like a flower, sitting on a lettuce leaf. *Did she just make a simple ham sandwich into a work of culinary art?*

"Thanks. Looks good." Gauge toted the plate to the dinette.

Aniyah laughed. "It's just a ham sandwich!"

"Doesn't matter. It was made by your talented hands, so there's definitely something special about it."

She rolled her eyes and shook her head. "Always with the flattery."

"Hey, I mean it." He sat down as she joined him with her own plate.

He took a bite of the sandwich. She was right. It was just a ham sandwich, but the thought of her being the one who prepared it made it taste even better. He looked across the table, briefly locking eyes with her as she chomped on her own helping. Breaking the stare, she set down her half-eaten sandwich and frowned.

"What's wrong? Don't like the sandwich?" He stopped eating as well.

She looked at him carefully. "How much trouble am I in, being around you?"

Gauge furrowed his brow. "What do you mean?"

"I've been thinking a lot about what you said about your clan having many enemies. What does that mean for me if I were to get involved with you? Will my life continuously be in danger?"

He swallowed a lump in his throat. *Does she honestly think that?* His heart pounded as he realized just how serious the situation was. He had to make the move on Axle and take over the Whitetide Streak. He had to restore the peace that had been lost when Axle came to power. He had to stop running and face his fear of failure. He had to do it for Aniyah. "No, your life won't continuously be in danger. I'll make sure of that," he finally replied. "I intend to stop this for good. It's a complicated matter that involves several pieces. My brother Axle may not have friends, but I do. I won't be alone when it all goes down. I'm going to fight. For you. For us."

Her eyes widened slightly. "Don't do anything stupid. You're the first guy I've met who really seems legit in everything he says and does. I don't want to lose a guy like you."

His heart swelled. She cared—for him.

He smiled. "You won't lose me. When the smoke has cleared, I want you to come stay with me."

She tilted her head. "Stay with you? But I have a business to run. I have my own life."

"Would you stay with me if I found you your own bakery?"

Her face brightened. "Maybe. But the bakery would not be why I would want to stay with you. If I can continue to do the things that I love and still have you in my life, then I would be all for it."

His smile broadened. Having been put on patrolling duties during his time in the clan, he knew of the small towns that the Whitetide's territory overlapped. He was certain that some shops where he could negotiate a rental deal were vacant. "Okay. I'll keep that in mind. In the meantime, don't you worry."

Sighing, she pushed her plate aside and stood. Walking over to the big window in the living area, she hugged herself.

Gauge watched her and suddenly lost his appetite. He swept to her side and rested a hand at the small of her back for reassurance. "Hey. I told you not to worry."

"I should've known that it was too good to be true, that finally finding an amazing guy like you would have strings attached."

Gauge clenched his jaw. He spun her around and placed both hands on her cheeks, making her look at him. "There are no strings attached. I told you. I will make sure the Silverfangs—and any other clan, for that matter—never bother you again." He hardened his gaze as he stared deep into her intriguing eyes. He sensed her fear and mix of emotions. The wolves had traumatized her. They'd put a target on her back and would search unrelentingly for her. He couldn't allow that—he wouldn't. What Diesel refused to do, Gauge would do himself. Rather than trying to persuade others to fight his battles, Gauge had to show his oppressors just how much of an alpha he really was.

Gauge continued to stare into Aniyah's eyes, his desire to create a future with her becoming clear in his mind. The day of reckoning with Axle was coming sooner than he'd thought.

"Our meeting wasn't an accident," he finally told Aniyah, drawing the pad of his thumb down her cheek. "If you'll have me, I'll give you everything a beautiful queen like you wants and deserves."

Her breath hitched. He could hear her quick heartbeat. Her scent empowered him, urging his tiger to escape. He slowly drew his face closer to hers and paused halfway. Her eyelids flickered downward, to his lips. His tiger was one second away from breaking through.

Finally, she pressed her lips to his, claiming him first. He cupped the sides of her face with his hands and returned the kiss. Moaning softly, she grabbed a fistful of his shirt.

Her taste, her heat, her need… everything about her unleashed the desire of his caged tiger. He tore her away from the window and guided her to the couch. The colors in his vision transitioned back and forth from muted to vibrant as he struggled to maintain control of his beast. As he crawled on top of her, he felt her tugging at his shirt, and he briefly broke the kiss to shed his clothing then help her out of hers. His lips locking back onto hers, he got a second helping of her delectable desire, and the ever-increasing musky scent of her need filled his nostrils. His mouth traveled down the length of her neck, kissing and licking her smooth, dark skin. Everything about her was beautiful—perfect.

"That… That feels good. You feel so good…" she whispered, closing her eyes.

"You taste good." Gauge smirked then sucked on her neck. He moved his tongue down her collarbone. "I want you as my mate. I want you to be mine."

Her eyes shot open. "Y-Your mate?"

"Yes." He let out a low growl. "You are the beautiful queen I've needed in my life."

She blushed. "You're such a charmer." She slowly drew her finger up his sternum. "I'll be your mate. I'll be everything you want me to be."

He grabbed the finger and brought the back of her hand to his lips. "I want you to be the woman you are right now." He dropped her hand and lowered the straps of her red lace bra. As the front clasps were undone, the garment fell away, revealing Aniyah's healthy, round breasts. His dick went ramrod straight. He leaned in and indulged in her nipples, teasing them with flicks of his tongue.

"Mmm… D-Don't stop," she whimpered.

He sucked hard and greedily on her nipples until they protruded and hardened. Then he flicked them with his tongue again.

Moaning, she squirmed, but he held her down.

"Stay," he ordered.

Her body trembled beneath him. Parting her thighs with his knees, he caught the scent of her wetness.

His dick throbbed. Spurts of pre-cum drizzled from the tip. *Damn! The crazy things this woman does to me!*

He sat up and moved his hands along the thick curves around her hips and midsection. She was delicious. He thought about how much sexier she would be if she bore his children someday.

He let out a breath as the thought of her being pregnant nearly made him cum too soon. He wanted a taste of her nectar first. He would hold out for her until he'd tasted all of her. He drew farther down her body then buried his face between her legs and licked her juices from her thighs and around her pussy.

"Shit!" she cried out, attempting to squirm again, but he kept her pinned in place.

"I said, 'Stay,'" he growled. Then he slid his tongue around her clit and flicked her pink pearl, which quickly hardened from his ministrations.

"Ungh… so… ama… zing…" she croaked in a shaky voice.

He drove his tongue into her and swirled it around her walls, lapping up every drop of her juice.

He sucked and slurped until he could no longer take the growing pain in his dick. *Fuck. Need to fill her up right now.*

He gave her clit a final kiss before pulling back. Then he sat on the couch, pulled her onto his lap, and guided her hips over his thick, erect dick. Moaning, he slid into her easily. He kneaded the supple flesh of her hips then reached around to her ass and palmed two handfuls of her soft cheeks. He ground into her in a slow and steady rhythm, his breathing ragged. The sweat of their bodies made them stick together like glue as they moved. Her full breasts bounced happily in front of his face, and he took one of her nipples in his mouth. Faster, he drove her, sucking hungrily on her long, hard nipple while he relished the feel of every curve and every jiggle and vibration of their movements. He pumped her deeper, the tip of his thick cock grazing her cervix.

"There… there it is…" he murmured, his voice hovering between human and beast as he fought to keep his tiger from escaping.

Her pussy clenched around his member, and she cried out her climax.

Gauge let out a satisfied growl, feeling her hot juice envelop his dick. His mind went blank. His hips gyrated faster, grinding her harder as he drew out the last of her orgasm.

"Yes… That's it, baby… All of it…" he said in praise. Then he held her close and, with a long groan, exploded every ounce of his energy into her. She gasped, and her body shook while he settled his throbbing dick against her cervix and emptied every drop into her. He filled her until her pussy overflowed and leaked out hot white streams of his cum. He sighed and relaxed as Aniyah collapsed on top of him.

"Ho… ly… Fucking… shit…" she gasped between breaths.

He kissed her tenderly on her forehead. "There is one last thing, my tigress…"

"Hmm?"

He stroked one side of her neck with the pads of his fingers then leaned over and kissed a small spot between her neck and collarbone. Her skin was warm, her taste still delectable. "I'm going to mark you as my mate."

She stared at him, half-aroused, half-confused. "Will it hurt?"

"Maybe a little."

She grimaced a little. "This is a shifter ritual, isn't it?"

"Yes."

"Mmm… Okay. Go ahead. I'm ready. Make me yours."

He took a bite, just deep enough to draw blood. She let out a gasp, and her whole body twitched. The taste of her blood nearly gave his tiger a second wind, but he managed to restrain it as he licked the wound closed, sealing their bond, confirming she was his.

He lay behind her on the couch, pulling her to him and wrapping his arms around her in a warm cuddle. Exhausted but wholly satisfied, he stared at the scar on her neck, visible enough to other shifters' keen eyes. He kissed her cheek and whispered in her ear, "Now, you're mine."

Closing her eyes, she smiled and whispered back. "That felt… kind of arousing."

He smirked. "Sometimes pain can be arousing."

"I would love to explore more of these shifter rituals."

"You will in due time. With this bond, you are now part of my world." He shut his eyes and listened to their synced heartbeats. "I need to tell you something important. I am going away until after the next full moon to deal with the Silverfang Pack. I am gathering allies."

Her body tensed, and she opened her eyes. "What?"

"I will be back for you, Aniyah. I have marked you as my mate."

She fell silent for a moment. "Why do you have to do this? What if you don't come back?"

Hearing the sadness in her voice, he felt his throat tighten. "I'm not going to think about 'what if.' I want to see you again. I want to have a family with you. But I have to do this. It is the only chance I have to restore honor to my clan and to become the new alpha. And you will rule beside me as my queen." He kissed the scar on her neck.

"I don't like this, Gauge... I have a bad feeling..."

"You must understand. This is how things are in the shifter circles. It is how my kind survives."

She sighed. "Yeah... I get it... Come back, please. I've been hurt by men all my life, men that I've poured my very heart into. Please don't do it to me again..."

A wave of determination burned away the anxiety in his chest. Now, more than ever, he had to fight for her. She was the only thing that mattered.

She was his everything.

CHAPTER 7

Two weeks later…

GAUGE PULLED UP BESIDE BARRON and flipped down his motorcycle's kickstand. He stared up at a massive wood-and-stone mansion that stood before a backdrop of tall maples, oaks, and birches painted with the colorful gradients of autumn. The massive structure looked more like a luxury hunting lodge than a personal dwelling. They were at the Blacktail estate, located deep in the Appalachians, in the heart of Blacktail territory. Gauge's newly repaired motorcycle had survived the rough ten-hour trip, much to his relief.

Gauge's heart pounded, as it was the first time he had set foot on Blacktail territory. Though they were allies, he knew that one wrong move—one wrong thing said—would sever that alliance. He respected the Blacktails for their undying loyalty to the Whitetide Streak during his aunt Evaline's rule, and he hoped he would find that same loyalty among them one more time.

For two weeks, Gauge had stayed with Barron in his townhome just outside New Rochford. He never traveled back to the city, for fear of running into Diesel again. He feared his older brother out of respect. That was his territory, after all. But Gauge's business was no longer with him.

Being away from Aniyah for so long was torture. But Gauge required the time away to train and prepare for the battle ahead. He'd stayed in contact with her, however, calling and texting her almost every day to tell her how much he missed her. That was all he could do for the time being, until his task was complete.

"Home sweet home," Barron said, dismounting his "Big Boss" V-8 chopper in front of the mansion.

A small black image moved beyond the trees then disappeared. Gauge tensed. The scent of bears surrounding him intensified.

"C'mon." Barron made a small head gesture then headed up the gravel walkway.

Gauge walked close beside his friend. He glanced over his shoulder and spotted two black bears walking around his bike, sniffing and examining it carefully. He swallowed a lump in his throat and turned to his friend. "You, uh… sure everything's cool with your family?" he asked.

"If it wasn't, I wouldn't have brought you here."

"Ehh… yeah… right." Gauge rubbed the back of his head.

They reached the grand entrance. Gauge stared at the ornate, pawprint-shaped golden knocker that hung on the rustic wooden door.

Barron knocked, and moments later, an adolescent boy with dark, shaggy hair answered. His gaze bounced between Barron and Gauge, and his sandy-beige skin lit up as bright as the sun.

"Whoa! Uncle Bear-Bear's back!" He beamed then gave the big man a hug.

Barron smiled, returning the hug, and patted him on the back. "Hey, Jacoby. Holding down the fort, I see."

The boy's smile broadened, and he puffed his chest out. "Sure am! How am I doing?"

"Just fine." He ruffled his hair.

Jacoby's eyes settled on Gauge, and he tilted his head. "Who're you?"

He gave the kid a small salute. "I'm Gauge, a friend of your uncle."

"This is my bro!" Barron playfully grabbed Gauge in a headlock and mussed his hair.

"Oof!" Gauge laughed, unable to break out of his friend's solid hold.

Barron liked to embarrass him like that sometimes, ever since they were young.

"Hey, man! Cut it out!" Gauge said.

Grinning, Barron released him.

Jacoby laughed, too, and stepped aside to let them in.

Gauge stood in the foyer, admiring the warm, cozy wooden-themed interior. High windows and ceilings and rustic furniture that spoke of the outdoors complemented the luxurious home, which was fit for a bear clan.

"Where's Bossman today?" Barron asked the boy.

Jacoby nudged his head backward. "Out in the courtyard with Grandma. I think they're gonna take Marla to the training grounds in a bit."

He nodded. "Thanks." He motioned for Gauge to follow.

Gauge shuffled beside him and snickered. "'Uncle Bear-Bear'?" he teased his friend.

"Hey, according to him, I'm the *cool* uncle." Barron flashed a grin.

Gauge's smile fell slightly. Seeing Barron's positive relationship with his family made him envious. The estranged relationship Gauge had with his siblings and clan was like an unforgiving nightmare. It made him more determined to make things right and restore what his family had lost.

They entered the courtyard, a massive garden with waterfalls, koi ponds, colorful flora, and a long, winding flagstone path. Gauge took in the scenery as though he'd stepped into a dream.

"Whoa, man. This is nice," he said in awe.

"It was my favorite place to hang out as a kid," Barron said.

They reached the end of the path, where an older woman and little girl sat together at a wrought iron bistro table, reading a children's book. A larger, burly man stood by, watching them and smiling under his thick black beard.

"And the rude woman leapt out of bed with a fright," the woman and little girl read together in a staccato, sing-song voice, "and ran to the window with all her might. The three bears chased—mad as all heck! But she fell from the window and broke her neck. She was dead, of course, to cause trouble no more. So be kind to your neighbor when you come to their door!"

"The end!" The girl beamed a jack-o'-lantern smile. "Let's read it again, Gramma!"

"Maybe later, dear. It's almost time for your training."

Barron approached. The larger man swiveled his gaze at him, then it settled on Gauge.

"Hey, Mom. Pop..." Barron said, inclining his head.

The woman looked his way and grinned. Then she stood from her chair and approached him, arms extended. "Barron! How are you, son?"

Gauge moistened his lips and kept his head lowered. His eyes burned a little as he witnessed the heartfelt reunion, a feeling he'd never experienced himself. Instead of love, Gauge's family was full of unnecessary drama and pain. *When I'm alpha, that will change...*

A set of large boots appeared in front of him, followed by heavy breathing. Gauge snapped out of his thoughts and stared up at Barron's father—the Blacktail Clan's alpha—Jeremiah Austin. The man easily towered over him, and his broad, husky frame was as solid as a brick wall. He was a true mountain man. Gauge's throat tightened as the big man's pointed stare seemed to stab right through his soul.

"H-Hello, sir…" Gauge stammered, his voice cracking.

"Hmph…" He grunted and turned toward his mate. "Go take Marla to the field while we discuss business here."

She nodded and gathered the child. As she brushed past Gauge, she stopped, looked him up and down, and quirked a smile. "Hmm… Gauge Reed. You turned out to look like your father," she said.

Gauge raised his eyebrows at her. "Is that a good or bad thing?"

Her smile grew a little, and she continued down the path. "He had a big heart, much like his sister, Evaline."

The mention of his aunt drew mixed emotions of fear and sadness. Little by little, he was learning more about his family's impact on the other clans.

"Sit," Jeremiah said, gesturing toward the empty, two-seater bistro table.

Gauge did so without hesitation, and Barron plopped down across from him.

Jeremiah remained standing. Crossing his thick arms over his broad chest, he alternated his attention between Barron and Gauge.

"So, you're still gonna help, right, Pop?" Barron asked, breaking the awkward silence.

"I never said I would help. I said I would *talk*," he said in a gruff voice. "I'm not thrilled about helping any damned Whitetide." His annoyed gaze settled on Gauge.

Gauge took a deep breath, mustering the courage to speak to the foreboding alpha. "Hear me out, sir. I know my clan has made a lot of mistakes. I don't condone any of Axle's actions. That's why I came here on my own accord, seeking the help of allies. I plan to face Axle someday and take over as alpha. I'm going to restore the Whitetide Streak to the former glory you remember from when my Aunt Evaline ruled.

"But I need to take things in steps. Small battles. That's why I need to defeat the Silverfang alpha. Besides that, they almost killed someone very dear to me. I can't let that go. They have to pay. But I can't do it alone.

"This is the only way to prove my worthiness of the Whitetide throne and bring some respect back to my clan. The Silverfangs are a dangerous enemy to us. Axle tried to slay Xander, the alpha, but failed. But I intend to succeed. However, I can't very well take on a whole clan by myself."

The man stroked his thick beard in thought. "Hmph. You can't expect me to needlessly send people to their deaths when we do not know the current status of the enemy."

"Gauge and I have spent these past few weeks keeping tabs on them, Pop," Barron said. "I did some scouting. Their numbers are nine. The next full moon is in a couple days. That is when they will do their running."

"And that is when we strike," Gauge finished.

The Blacktail alpha scowled under his beard. "We are fourteen strong, not including the cubs. I can't very well send everyone off to fight when we need to keep our own territory secure."

Gauge sighed. "Anyone you can spare, sir, would be helpful."

"You got me at least, man," Barron said to Gauge with a curt nod.

Gauge smiled back at his friend.

Jeremiah grunted. "I'll see what I can do."

"Pop, Gauge is trying to take over the Whitetide Streak. Wouldn't you rather have *him* as a leader than Axle?"

He regarded his son with slight disgust. "I'd rather have a leader who makes *allies*, not enemies."

"Give me a chance, sir," Gauge pleaded. "I promise to make things right."

The alpha's gaze flicked to Gauge for a moment, then he turned and headed for the courtyard's exit. "We'll see."

CHAPTER 8

Two days later…

GAUGE HAD NEVER DREAMED HE might see the day he would be traveling alongside a posse of Blacktail riders across Appalachia. Jeremiah led the way, riding his own monstrous "Big Boss" V-8, which made his son's version look like a harmless scooter. He'd recruited seven of his strongest warriors—enough to even the Silverfang's numbers—who were also thirsty for battle.

Their bikes packed with light camping gear and supplies, the group tore down the roads and highways with a vicious, rumbling roar of pipes like an approaching tumultuous storm. As for Gauge, he intended to rain down death on the Silverfang wolves.

Gauge couldn't stop smiling as he rode alongside his best friend, surrounded by the rest of the Blacktail clan. The ten-hour trip felt shorter for Gauge, perhaps due in part to him still being awed by the bear clan's support. Despite the Whitetide Streak's reputation, tarnished by Axle's poor leadership, the Blacktails were willing to give Gauge a chance. In the two days he'd stayed with the clan in their territory, he had earned their trust. He'd slept in their guest room and eaten meals at their table. They treated him like their very own—much better treatment than Gauge's own family. A small part of him wished he and Barron were actual brothers. Growing up in a loving, tight-knit family like Barron's seemed like everything Gauge always wanted but could never have. Perhaps one day, when he had his own family, he could make that dream come true.

His thoughts traveled to Aniyah. Though he called her every day, he could hear the sadness in her voice. She'd been staying busy all this time with an influx of new customers. She was running a booming business, and Gauge wondered if she was reaching a point at which she had to choose between him and the business. When everything was over, he intended to go straight back to her and hold her tight, to remind her how much he cared for her—how much he *loved* her.

But he would never get that chance if order wasn't restored.

They reached the edge of the Cedarstone Heights town limits and parked in a dirt lot of a lively motorcycle bar. At nine o'clock at night, the music and festivities inside the bar were just getting started. The Blacktails parked together in a tight group, away from the bar patrons' bikes. Gauge dismounted and joined them. The group retreated into the thick forest and set up a small camp.

"Moonset starts at eleven ten tonight," Barron explained to his father. "The Silverfang will be doing their running at that time." He took out his cell phone and pulled up the map of the area.

Jeremiah peered at the phone then addressed the other members. "LeAnna and Shep, you two take the west point. Mitchell and Bethany, cover the east. Barron, Gauge, take the south point. I will cover the north," he explained, pointing at spots on the map. "Do not engage until we have them corralled at this point." He indicated on the map the middle of the forest, next to Cedarstone River.

"And Xander is mine," Gauge added. His gaze swiveled back and forth at the members, hoping nobody would oppose.

The group made their final preparations. By ten forty-five, they were all shifted and ready.

Gauge and Barron ran toward the south point. The cool night air flowing through his nostrils, Gauge felt his heart race as anxiety and adrenaline took over. Fifteen minutes later, they reached the south point and settled there, hiding themselves amongst the underbrush.

Gauge crouched low to the ground and stared into the endless sea of birches and oaks surrounding him. Faint wolf howls echoed in the distance. A shiver ran down his spine.

Barron's voice projected into his mind. *"Ready to do this, man?"*

Gauge nodded once, his heart continuing to pound. Greystone Creek was just across Cedarstone River, beyond the great ridge that separated them. He was merely a stone's throw away from taking the Whitetide throne.

"Yeah…" he replied at last.

They waited in silence, listening and watching the position of the moon to determine the time. Soon, the faint, distant howling of wolves intensified. Gauge noted a different pitch of the howls, indicating the start of their ritual run.

"Let's go," Gauge ordered. With his body still crouched, he quietly slinked through the underbrush.

Barron followed closely behind, his large, burly form making it impossible for him to sneak. His ears perked, Gauge followed the howling sounds, which were coming from the west. The triumphant voices grew louder and more panicked the closer Gauge and Barron approached.

"Sounds like Shep and LeAnna have started the chase," Barron projected.

Gauge focused his keen eyes ahead. Several pairs of glowing yellow dots danced in the distance. Memories swarmed his mind, of that fateful night he'd first met Aniyah. Growling, he pursued the yellow dots. A pack of nine wolves rushed toward him like an approaching wave. The images of the wolves became clear as they neared, and Gauge spotted the largest one in front. The massive wolf stood close to six feet tall, rivaling Barron's brawny stature. Hanging around his neck was a wooden ring attached to a corded necklace.

The alpha's ring... Xander Silverfang... Gauge mused, his gaze pinning the piece of jewelry.

A bear's ferocious roar boomed behind the wolves, sending the group into a frenzy. Xander looked toward Gauge and howled.

Gauge roared back in challenge then ran straight at him.

Shep and LeAnna soon appeared behind the pack, and the other wolves reversed course toward the east.

Xander, seemingly unfazed, took Gauge's challenge, not straying from his path.

"Yo! We gotta stick to the plan!" Barron said in Gauge's mind.

Gauge narrowed his eyes. The plan was to corral the *whole* pack. But Xander had decided to throw a wrench into that plan. *"I can't let him get away,"* he told his friend.

"Gauge! What about—"

"Take care of the rest of the pack. I got this." Gauge's throat tightened as he projected those words.

Xander split from his pack and ran the opposite direction, deeper into the woods.

Shep and LeAnna continued pursuing the pack.

Barron hesitated, casting Gauge a brief glance, and sent, *"You better know what you're doing, man."* Then he turned and ran after his clan mates.

Gauge wasn't entirely sure what he was doing, but he knew he had only one chance to defeat the alpha. Maybe he was headed straight for a trap, but he couldn't take the chance of Xander escaping again. He pursued the large wolf at top speed. Aniyah's face flashed in his mind, a constant reminder of what he was fighting for—whom he was fighting for. That determination incited an extra burst of energy that drew him only inches away from the wolf's tail.

Xander suddenly switched directions and whipped his body around, out of Gauge's line of attack.

Gauge slid to a brutal stop, his body knocking against sharp rocks and jagged pieces of wood on the ground. Grunting, he struggled back to his feet and faced the Silverfang alpha.

The great wolf bared his canines and snarled, streams of drool oozing from his mouth. *"Fuck you Whitetide scum for invading our territory! Disrupting our sacred running! You will pay for this! You and the rest of your clan of cowards!"* he projected into Gauge's mind.

Gauge narrowed his eyes, feeling his burning, bestial rage coursing through his veins. *"I will do what should have been done a long time ago—what my brother failed to do. You will not torment us anymore."*

Xander charged at him, his head down, and rammed Gauge's body against the side of a large rock.

Gauge landed on his back with a grunt, the wind knocked out of him. Xander stood over him, jaws opened. His golden eyes flashed once.

Gritting his teeth, Gauge swiped his paw at the side of Xander's face. The wolf's head snapped to the side, and four deep, bloody gashes appeared. Growling, Xander dove his maw toward Gauge's neck. In a split second, Gauge caught sight of Xander's exposed underbelly and raked his back claws through it. Xander flinched, letting out a pained whine, then took hold of Gauge's neck in recoil.

Gauge widened his eyes. Fiery pain shot through the side of his neck, and breathing became difficult. *No... I can't fail... Aniyah...* he thought as the world around him grew darker. He saw her face again, heard her pleading voice:

"Come back, please. I've been hurt by men all my life. Men that I've poured my very heart into. Please don't do it to me again..."

No, he'd vowed that he would never hurt her, that she would be his tigress.

Fight, damn it...

Then, Aniyah's image disappeared, and he saw Cammy.

"You're not ready," his sister's voice echoed in his mind.

Gauge snarled. *I am fucking ready.*

"Prove it."

Gauge tasted blood. He was losing air fast. He channeled the remaining rage and energy of his beast and, with his last desperate attempt, reached out for Xander's throat with his front claws. He plunged them deep into the wolf's flesh like a pincushion. He kicked his back legs against Xander's underbelly, faster, repeatedly, as though he was spasming. His claws raked and tore deeper through the wolf's tough skin, to the bone. The wound widened to a large gaping hole that poured blood and innards like a waterfall.

Xander's hold on Gauge's neck weakened. His eyes widened and cast Gauge a deathly stare.

"You... have not... won. The Dessar... shall rise..." Xander's weak voice projected into Gauge's mind. The wolf exhaled his final breath, and his body went limp and still.

Gauge kept his claws lodged in Xander's flesh a little while longer. When he was certain the wolf was dead, he slowly retracted his claws. Then, with a grunt, Gauge rolled Xander's body off of himself. He took a slow, unsteady breath. The scent of his and Xander's blood assaulted his nose. He checked himself and grimaced at the sight of blood and gore covering him as if in a bad horror flick. He was a mess, but he was alive.

I did it. I defeated him, he thought. But still something bugged him—Xander's dying words. *The Dessar? Oh, fuck...* The Dessar Pack, led by their alpha, Zephyr Beckett, was the strongest and highest wolf order in the region. Besides being allied with the other wolf clans, the Dessar also offered them protection. During the days of Evaline's rule, the Whitetide Streak had managed a mutual relationship with them, especially since their territories were so close. But when Axle came to power, that relationship was shattered, and they had become a long-standing enemy. Now, that sentiment seemed to be permanent after the threats made to Gauge and Anyiah's life.

The ground tremored beneath him as several footsteps thundered nearer. Gauge lifted his head and looked toward the sounds. Jeremiah and the rest of the Blacktails approached, bloodied and exhausted. All seven bears were accounted for—they, too, had been victorious.

Jeremiah halted and stared. Then Barron rushed to Gauge's side.

"Gauge!" Barron projected in a frantic voice. He nudged Gauge's body with his nose.

He groaned and slowly rolled on his side. Cringing, he projected, *"I'm okay…"*

Barron growled. *"You're not okay. You're bleeding out of your neck, man! I'm taking you back to the camp."* He lowered his body, shimmied Gauge onto his back, and rose.

Gauge closed his eyes for a moment, relieved to feel the comfort of Barron's soft fur rather than jagged rocks and a wolf corpse.

Jeremiah approached Xander's body, sniffed it, and snarled. Then he turned to Gauge, his yellow-glowing eyes burning with rage.

"He's dead," Gauge projected to the Blacktail alpha.

"You strayed from the plan!" Jeremiah growled. *"We were supposed to hold off attacking until the wolves were corralled at center point!"*

Gauge let out a pained moan. *"Well, things didn't go as planned when Xander broke away and fled."*

Barron growled then projected a message to his father, and Jeremiah sneered at Gauge. Afterward, Barron began his slow and careful trek back to camp. The other bears parted a path to allow Barron to walk ahead.

"Is your dad still pissed at me?" Gauge projected to his friend once they were well on their way.

"Eh, he'll get over it. I told him if he wants to talk more about it, then he should do it at camp. We won tonight, and that's what counts. The Silverfangs are no more. Now, you will be able to claim your alpha title."

Gauge's body jostled atop Barron's back. He stared at the passing trees looming in the eerie darkness. *"I don't know, man... Something... Something's not right..."*

"What do you mean?"

"Before he died, Xander mentioned the Dessar..."

Barron fell silent a moment. *"As in the Dessar Clan?"*

Gauge nodded.

"You've gotta be shitting me..."

They returned to camp, and Barron laid Gauge in one of the pop-up tents. Gauge concentrated on the wound afflicting his neck. Thanks to his innate shifter abilities, it was already healing, slowly but surely, but the pain didn't subside. His battle wounds were still too great for him to concentrate on his shifting. So he simply remained where he lay, silent and still.

He thought about the night's battle. He was victorious, yet Gauge felt like he failed somehow again. He'd made a choice that he thought was the right one, but like many other choices he'd made in his life, it had backfired in his face. His deep-seated focus on killing Xander had blinded him to the fact that his selfish actions made him no different from Axle.

Damn it. What am I doing all this for? He thought. *I'm trying to make a difference, and all I keep doing is fucking things up. This is not the way to get allies. Aunt Evaline would tear into my ass if she were here right now.*

The Blacktail bears returned. The beastly growls were soon replaced by coherent speech as they assumed their human forms.

Several minutes later, Jeremiah poked his head into Gauge's tent. The big man wore a deep scowl beneath his dark beard.

Gauge lifted his head, took one look at him, and lay his head back down. *"Look, I'm sorry, all right? When Xander split, I had to react..."* he said telepathically to the man.

Jeremiah grunted. "A leader sticks to the plan," he said aloud.

"But sometimes, things don't go as planned. I'm sure you're no stranger to that, right?"

"That's not the point. Your carelessness could have cost lives. That is not how alliances are formed."

Gauge hung his head and sighed. *"Yes, sir, and I'm sorry. It won't happen again."*

His stare hardened. "We did you a favor, Gauge Reed. Now, you owe us."

"I know. I haven't forgotten. I'm going to face my brother next. I will show him proof of the alpha's death with—" Gauge blinked. *"Shit! I forgot to swipe the ring off Xander's corpse!"*

Jeremiah's scowl lifted. He reached into his jeans pocket and pulled out a corded necklace with a wooden ring tied to it. "You mean this?"

CHAPTER 9

Aniyah stared insistently at the lit-up screen on her phone amid a backdrop of muted darkness. The full moon had passed a few days before, but Gauge was not back at her side like he'd promised. The long text message he'd written to her three days before offered some comfort, but she missed his warmth, his touch.

At two in the morning, she lay in bed, unable to sleep. It had been one of many sleepless nights since Gauge left. The past week had been shitty all around, since she'd eventually fallen too ill to work on clients' orders. She'd gotten two cancellations as a result, something rare in her business. But she'd gotten too weak to stand, much less work. The feeling of vertigo hit her head like a brick. And the porcelain god had quickly become her best friend.

She read Gauge's message again. He was coming home soon, but he didn't specify when. She yearned for her tiger-man more than ever, when she felt so alone and confused.

A sharp pain stabbed her abdomen, followed by a queasy feeling in her stomach. She jumped out of bed and raced to the bathroom. She stumbled onto her knees in front of the toilet as though kneeling before the great altar of the porcelain god, ready to confess her sins. At other times, she'd experienced this feeling, but it was never this severe. Finally, she hurled her offering—part of that night's dinner— into the bowl and leaned back against the wall. A chill ran up her spine as her skin touched the cold tile wall. Her brain swarmed with mixed feelings. She didn't want to believe what this feeling could have been—at least, not right then.

Am I really *ready?* She wondered. Thinking about the situation with Gauge still made her feel worlds apart from him. There was so much she didn't understand about his world—shifter society—but she was more than willing to accept that new life. Gauge had been shielding her from the dangers of shifter battles and politics, but she wanted to be a part of it, to feel his pains and struggle and to understand him more as his mate. But he was too damned stubborn to listen, and he cared too damn much for her.

She slowly got up and trudged back to her bedroom. She gingerly swiped up her discarded phone and plopped back into bed with it. The screen lit up once again, revealing Gauge's last text, which she'd read and reread over and over. At last, her eyes grew heavy, and she fell into a deep sleep.

As quickly as she had closed her eyes, midmorning had already come. Sunlight creeped over her face, rousing her from what felt like a short power nap. The fact that she'd been dreaming about Gauge didn't help.

Gauge! She perked up and groped for her phone, which sat on her night table. She checked the screen—no new messages—and deflated. Groaning, she dragged herself out of bed, showered and got dressed, and prepared to take on the day. The pain in her midsection was largely gone, and she used that opportunity to tackle some client work. One was a triple-layer cake order for a client's retirement party later that evening. Another client had ordered a dozen cake pops. Aniyah skimmed the ingredient list, hoping she had everything she needed.

As she was taking out pots, pans, and utensils, her phone suddenly buzzed on the counter. She jolted and dove for the phone. The screen lit up with a new message from Gauge:

more fmly shit... miss u... --Gauge

Aniyah's heart sank as she read the message over and over again. *Gone again...* The message sounded rushed. He wasn't coming back that day, probably. And nobody knew when he would. The initial thought of becoming Gauge's mate sounded exciting, that she would have someone who cared deeply for her to also be there for her. But these shifter matters were far more in-depth, which made her wonder if being a part of his world was really all that it was cracked up to be.

CHAPTER 10

Gauge rode the nearly four-hour trip nonstop on his motorcycle from the Blacktail estate all the way to Greyson Creek. In three years, Gauge hadn't set foot in the place he'd once called home. Since Axle's deadly ultimatum that forced Gauge to leave, life had changed for Gauge. He'd gained a mate, along with the courage to face his fear and defend his honor. He was ready for what came next.

Gauge parked his motorcycle at the edge of the woods, where a faint dirt path led deeper into the trees to his former home. Entering the woods, Gauge immediately picked up the scents of numerous wolves. He clenched his jaw. *Am I too late? Has the Dessar Clan's takeover already begun?* It was only a matter of time before the Whitetide Streak was obliterated, if it hadn't already been.

Gauge hustled down the path he'd always taken during his patrol shifts. The scent of wolves overpowered the other tigers'. The closer he got to his home, the stronger it got. He reached a clearing, where a large log cabin sat. In the distance, beyond the trees, Lake Greyson sparkled in the morning light. The sight triggered memories of his childhood, when he and his siblings used to play in the lake. Life had been carefree back then.

Those days will never come again, Gauge thought, approaching the cabin. Everything seemed quiet—a little *too* quiet. He glanced toward the curtained windows but saw no movement. He looked around, concentrating his senses on the area, his tiger becoming fully aware.

The hairs on his arm stood on end as he felt something approaching from above. His muted tiger senses caught wind of something big descending. He instinctively dodged the incoming attack, his startled tiger rousing quickly in anger.

A large golden tiger arose and locked its sights on Gauge. Very few golden tigers existed in the world. The last one Gauge had met was killed in a wolf raid. This tiger didn't smell familiar. *Has another joined the family since my short absence?*

The tiger's eyes emanated an icy-blue glow as the beast slowly crept closer. Gauge fell onto all fours and shifted. His powerful body ripped through his clothes.

The golden tiger stopped. Eyes narrowed, it projected a telepathic message to Gauge. *"You have five seconds to state your business here, trespasser."*

Gauge lowered his body in a nonthreatening stance. His battle was not with the golden tiger. *"I am Gauge Reed. I've come back to challenge your 'leader,' Axle."*

"'Come back'?" The tiger bared its fangs. *"So you are the one Axle spoke of, the weak coward who ran away. You will have to go through me to get to him."*

Gauge growled. *"My fight is with my brother, not you. I have come to make things right and prepare the clan for what is coming. I defeated the Silverfang alpha, something Axle failed to do."* He lifted his head, revealing the necklace with the alpha's ring tied to it.

The muscles in the tiger's body flexed. *"Liar! You will never see Axle."* In a flash, he pounced on Gauge.

Pinned by the tiger's great weight, Gauge struggled to move the beast, but the tiger was solid muscle. The tiger swiped at Gauge's face with its claws extended. Gauge watched the claws come dangerously close to his face. *Not again,* he thought.

With all his strength, Gauge used his body to heave the other tiger off. He rolled to his feet and tackled the golden tiger. He sank his teeth into the other tiger's neck and tightened his jaws. Gauge felt the other tiger struggle beneath him, but he remained strong. *"I'm not here to fight you,"* Gauge projected to his opponent.

The tiger made another fruitless attempt to throw him off, but he was losing breath fast. Gauge's ears flicked at the faint sounds of the cabin's door opening.

"I'm here, Gauge. Let him go."

Gauge froze at the sound of Axle's voice. He looked up briefly to see Axle's human form, a tall but husky man with short dark-brown hair. His matching brown eyes looked daggers at Gauge as he stood before them with his thick lumberjack arms crossed over his broad chest.

Gauge unclasped his jaws from the golden tiger's neck. The tiger flopped to the ground, barely breathing. Gauge stared at his brother, eyes narrowed, and crouched into a low stance, ready to pounce.

Axle lowered to the ground and assumed his tiger form. His body was slightly bigger than Gauge's, his muscles more defined. Gauge's heart pounded furiously. *This is really happening.*

"I warned you what would happen if you returned," Axle projected into Gauge's mind, slowly walking in a circle around him.

Gauge followed him, his tail lashing in anticipation. *"I know. That's why I'm here."*

"To die?"

Gauge narrowed his eyes and snarled. *"To take back what's rightfully mine."*

"You couldn't defeat me before, and you won't do it now."

"I defeated the Silverfang alpha and bear his ring. I am more than capable of defeating you now."

Axle glanced at the ring and sneered. *"How...? You could not have possibly—"*

"I know what's happening here, brother," Gauge interrupted, not feeding into his brother's stalling. *"With the threat of the Dessar clan and the other wolves. You've dishonored our family's name for the last time."*

Axle let out a low growl in response. *"Unlike you and Diesel, I did not run like a scared, weak cub."*

"I left to find someone worthy to defeat you. But it seemed I left for nothing. The only person who can defeat

you is me. And I've learned how to do exactly that. The wolves are closing in on this place. They have threatened not only my life but the life of someone who has now become my mate. That means war."

Axle snorted. "You *have a mate?"*

"I do. Are you still struggling to keep your mates because you're so damned insecure?"

"Fuck you!" Axle's muscles tensed.

"Cammy was right. You're no leader. All you do is piss everyone off and start wars. She was right to leave."

A low growl rumbled from Axle's throat. "So now you're counseling with that stupid brat?"

Gauge bristled. As much as he despised Cammy's antics, he couldn't deny that she was more in tune with clan matters than he or any of his brothers. She was wise beyond her years, which she hid behind an innocent mask. In a way, she reminded him of their late aunt Evaline, the clan's last powerful matriarch. If Gauge had his way, he would give the throne to Cammy. But she had already made it clear long before that she wanted nothing to do with it.

"She has more class than you'll ever have," Gauge projected to his brother.

"She doesn't know shit about what's going on around here!" Axle retorted.

"*She knows a hell of a lot more than you.*" Gauge held his head up high. "*Stand down, Axle. This is your last warning.*"

Axle's eyes flashed a deep orange. "*Fuck you. Now you die!*" He lunged at Gauge.

Gauge's inner beast snapped, and in that moment, he saw only red. Axle pounced on him and knocked him to the ground. He snapped his jaws at Gauge and swiped at him with long, razor-sharp claws. Memories of the fight with Diesel flooded Gauge's mind, and he dodged his brother's incoming paws. *I can't go down like this...*

Gauge fought back. His claws were not as fearsome as Axle's, but his attacks were faster. He swiped at Axle's face and chest with expert precision. Blood trickled from the wounds, and Axle howled in pain. With all his strength, Gauge pushed Axle off him.

Axle landed against the trunk of a tree, shaking it violently. He yelped and let out a breath. Gauge and Axle struggled back to their feet then ran at each other. They clashed again, attacking with powerful bites. Gauge's streamlined body moved with ease, and he dodged most of Axle's attacks.

They tumbled and tussled on the ground, violently ripping up grass, weeds, and dirt amid their snarls and growls. Finally, Gauge managed to grab hold of Axle's throat, just as his brother's claw came dangerously close to his right eye. Gauge closed his eyes and clamped down on his brother's throat. Sweat beaded beneath his fur, and his body was exhausted. But he didn't let go.

Axle's body shuddered, his movements becoming slower as he lost consciousness quickly. Gauge squeezed harder, puncturing skin, and eventually tasted blood.

"I... yield..."

Gauge froze, hearing his brother's weak voice projected in his mind. In all his years, he'd never thought he would ever hear Axle say those two words.

Axle's breath hitched.

"Are you serious?" Gauge asked.

Axle gagged, his tongue rolling in the back of his throat. Then his body went limp.

Gauge released his brother's neck. *Fuck... Did I kill him?* He stared at his brother's body, looking for any slight movement. *That's what I wanted, wasn't it?* Gauge mused. Part of him felt no remorse, yet a small part of him sought a different kind of closure.

Several gasps and whispers sounded around him. Gauge looked up, ready to attack whoever was next but hoping his potential attackers were wise not to interfere. Seven young men had gathered around to observe the fighting in awe. Only one of them smelled familiar to Gauge. *Weston...* Gauge recognized the man's face and slim build. He'd once sported a buzz cut but had since grown his hair out to long dreadlocks. Gauge and Weston had been friends once, before Weston fell to Axle's tyranny.

The golden tiger stirred as well. Gauge let out a warning growl at all of them. He wouldn't hesitate to take them all on if they decided to attack.

"Gauge? That you, man?" Weston asked, holding his hands up in surrender.

Gauge let out a deeper growl and whipped his tail back and forth. Seeing the humans keeping their distance, Gauge concentrated and assumed his own human form. Fully nude and uncaring of his exposure, he sat beside Axle, whose tiger form still lay deathly still.

"Gauge!" Weston exclaimed. "Damn, I can't believe you came back!"

Gauge glared at his ex–best friend then concentrated on Axle. Gauge lifted his brother's head and felt for a pulse. His hands went clammy when he didn't feel one at first, then moments later, he detected a very faint vibration. Gauge exhaled in relief. Axle was alive. *Why am I happy about that?*

"Is he…?" one of the other men asked.

Weston held up a hand and motioned toward the golden tiger. "Go tend to Emery. Bring him inside."

Gauge watched the other six men sidle around his space. Hefting up the golden tiger and bringing him inside the cabin was a team effort. Finally, Gauge was alone with his brother and his former friend.

"You have every right to be upset, Gauge," Weston began, approaching slowly, "but what could I have done? Only Whitetide blood could be a true leader of this clan, and none of us had completed our running in order to be officially inducted as blood brothers."

Gauge raised an eyebrow. "You mean you are still on probationary status after all this time?"

Weston frowned. "Your brother's a real power monger. He wanted no one even close to making his defeat official. There were too many of us from different former clans. Even if one of us did defeat him, we would all be nameless, the clan dissolved. And we knew about the wolves threatening the area.

They were just waiting for that, among other things."

Gauge frowned and looked at his brother. The situation was worse than he'd thought. He could kill Axle now and carry on the Whitetide name. *That's what I want, right?* His emotional war betrayed him. Finally, his rational side broke up the fight. Perhaps the time had come for Axle to live with his own shame for a change.

"Axle, wake up," Gauge called.

The tiger stirred again and let out a weak rumbling growl in his throat. His eyelids fluttered and opened slightly, revealing their deep-ochre color.

Gauge stood and walked past Weston. "Bring him inside." As he walked toward the front door, reality suddenly hit him. He had defeated Axle. He'd done the impossible—all because he believed in himself. The clan was his now. He'd taken what was rightfully his. Gauge would let Axle live, but he would make his brother work hard to earn what little respect he could get back from his clan mates.

Inside, he found the other clan members in the main living area, gathered around the couch, where a man with short golden-brown hair lay under a blanket. The other men regarded Gauge warily. One of them tossed him a small blanket.

Gauge wrapped the blanket around his waist then observed the scene. "Has this clan been only you guys?"

One of the men nodded.

"No females?" Gauge blinked.

The men exchanged looks. "Cammy left a long time ago. Axle could never keep a female. And he'd threaten to kill us if we ever sought mates in order to challenge him."

Gauge sneered. "Well, as the new alpha, I'm redacting his stupid, insecure rule. Help rebuild the Whitetide legacy and strength. I want only the strongest females in this family, ones who can fight and defend just as effectively as all of you, if not better. Our war with the wolf clans who have resided so close to our territory—most notably, the Dessar—is not over. We need to make an example of them so the other clans will remain at bay."

The others nodded then exchanged looks of surprise and excitement.

Gauge continued trekking through the house. The sights and smells were still familiar to him, despite how long he'd been away. He headed upstairs to the master bedroom—Axle's former room. He unwrapped the blanket from around his waist and rummaged through the drawers for an extra set of clothes. The T-shirt and cargo shorts were a little big, but they would have to do for the moment.

Returning downstairs, Gauge discovered Weston had returned with Axle, who had managed to shift back to his human form. He sat naked in a chair, breathing a little slowly. His face was badly bruised, and his body was scarred and bleeding. Gauge frowned at his brother and chucked an extra blanket at him. It landed haphazardly on Axle's lap. Weston smoothed it out and covered him.

"All right," Gauge said, addressing everyone in the room. "Now that I seem to have gotten everyone in this clan gathered, here's the deal. We're going to work our asses off to secure what little land we have left to protect from the Dessar Pack. No excuses."

"So you're saying the ten of us are going to go up against a pack of thirty or so wolves?" one of the men asked.

Gauge shook his head at the shorter thin man. "No, Dayton. We fight alongside allies."

Weston snorted. "What allies?"

"That's part of the plan," Gauge replied. "I'm still working on it." He addressed everyone again.

"Look. Our territory stinks of wolf. The Dessar will be closing in on us faster than we can blink. I want double patrol around the perimeter. Everyone be prepared for a fight in the coming days. If all of you wish to become true and honorable Whitetide blood, then prove your loyalty. Fight for your name, your family. The future of this clan depends on you."

The looks of doubt and fear on most of their faces soon vanished once Gauge finished. But the Dessar could strike at a moment's notice, and there wasn't much time to prepare. Gauge had to work quickly.

CHAPTER 11

Aniyah stared at her latest edible creations, vanilla shortcake cupcakes, and they sparked a bittersweet feeling. While she knew her client would love them, Aniyah's empty feeling had grown. Another week had passed since Gauge had texted her about being delayed with more family matters. His messages were becoming fewer and further between since then, and the anxiety in her heart rose. *Is he hurt? Did he forget about me? Are these family matters consuming him so much that he's given up on our future?* Aniyah couldn't stop thinking about their conversation before he left. She hadn't regretted letting him claim her, and her pussy clenched just thinking about that beautiful night.

Our worlds are so vastly different. Are we even meant to be together? She wanted to tell him so much that she couldn't just convey through a phone text.

The more she thought about it, the more hesitation filled her heart. She wasn't sure she was ready to begin a new life and finally fulfill her dreams of running her own bakery. Even when Gauge first mentioned it, Aniyah had had a funny feeling that a price would have to be paid. That price was becoming a part of his clan, part of his world, which seemed to be in constant war. But in the short time she'd known him, he'd been nothing but considerate and sweet to her. No other man she'd met had ever given her as much love and respect as Gauge.

The rational side of her brain added to her fluster.

Are you seriously going to let a hot catch like him go?

Aniyah chewed her bottom lip.

Everything comes with a price, including happiness. How much are you willing to pay?

She closed her eyes for a moment and thought. No price was too great if it meant spending the rest of her life with a sexy, chivalrous tiger-man like Gauge. She was in her mid-thirties, and time was running out for her to make up her mind. Men like Gauge were few and far between lately.

She topped the cupcakes with bright-red cherries, finishing them off. She carefully placed the cupcakes into a decorative box and set it in her refrigerator to keep them cool. As she was cleaning up, her doorbell rang. At first, she thought one of her clients had come by, too eager to wait to get their order, but none of her clients had a habit of making surprise visits.

She opened the door, and her heart fluttered. Gauge was standing on her doorstep, dressed in black leather and a pair of matching motorcycle boots. He quirked a charming smile at her, the cute scar on his cheek appearing.

"Gauge…" she said breathlessly.

He took her hand and kissed its back. "Hey. Sorry I've been away for so long."

She blushed and stepped aside to let him in. "It… it's okay. I understand. Family business and all that."

Gauge closed the door behind himself and looked at her carefully. For several moments, they stared at each other.

Aniyah's pussy spasmed painfully, and she hoped he would kiss her right then and maybe do a little more. She swallowed, trying to keep her composure, and wrapped her arms around him. They stood in an embrace, and she leaned against him, her ear pressed to his chest. She listened to his fast-beating heart while relishing the gentle, soothing sensation of his fingers combing through her hair. Sparks ignited in her belly, and she wished they could relive the night she'd become his mate.

His body stiffened, and he broke the embrace. Both hands grasping her shoulders, he stared at her up and down then sniffed once. "You smell different," he said. Then his eyes widened slightly. "Are you…?"

Her throat tightened. *He knows? Of course he knows.* Gauge was a tiger who relied on his primal instincts. She lowered her head and slowly lifted the bottom of her shirt, revealing a subtle bump in her muffin top.

He let out a short gasp. His face glowing with pride, he sank to his knees and planted feather-soft kisses on her belly.

Her breath hitched. She'd missed the feel of his lips on her skin. Her pussy yearned for him to satisfy her needs once more. "G-Gauge…" she whispered.

He looked up at her with deep, loving eyes. "You're going to have our baby? You're going to give me an heir?"

One corner of her lips tugged upward into a smile. "I guess I am."

"You 'guess'?" He rose to his feet and pulled her back into his arms. "You have no idea how much I've missed the fuck out of you." He planted a deep, passionate kiss on her lips without mercy.

Completely caught off guard, Aniyah moaned against his lips. But her body melted under his energetic kiss. She could already taste his need. Her face grew hotter. Gauge's outdoor scent, mixed with the leather, drove her wild. Gauge's hands caressed down her curves before he situated them on her ass and gave her cheeks a tight squeeze. The unexpected jolt of passion drew out another delightful moan from her.

He held her tightly against him, and even through the leathers, she could feel his hard need. Breaking the kiss, she took a breath and regarded him with hooded eyes.

He pressed his forehead against hers and closed his eyes. "Hey. I need to tell you something," he murmured, his tone edged with concern. His soothing touch steeled with doubt. "I *have* to tell you something."

Her pussy revolted at his unexpected teasing. Curiosity overshadowed her need. Her heart beat steadily faster as reality began to set in. *He's serious, isn't he?* Many questions jumbled in her mind. "What is it?" she asked, hoping he hadn't given up on them already.

Gauge averted his gaze for a moment then sighed. "There is something big about to happen at home, and I don't know when I'll come back to you."

She blinked. "But you just came back! You're leaving again?"

"I must..."

"What's happening at home?"

"War. And our future."

She let out a small gasp. *"Our" future...* The words echoed in her mind, and she balled her fists. A spark of determination hit her like a bolt of lightning, and she finally made up her mind. *Enough of this shit.* If they were going to be bonded for life, she needed to become more involved in his world. "Gauge, I want to join you. Fight by your side."

Gauge shook his head. "No. I can't risk you—" He paused and placed a hand over her bump. "Or our child."

She shut her eyes for a moment, relishing his touch, but even she could sense his fear and concern. Then she took a deep breath and opened her eyes. "If we're going to make this work, then it's only right that I do."

"But you're a pastry chef, not a fighter." He gave her a hint of a smile. "I should be the one protecting you."

She blew a raspberry. "Please, I'm not a defenseless damsel. I played softball in college for two years. Put a bat in my hands, and I'll slug one out of the park."

His smile broadened. "I can believe it. Fuck. You are so amazing, Aniyah. Through all the shit I've had to deal with, I thought about you the entire time to keep my sanity. You're the reason why I'm not dead."

She grimaced. "Gee, thanks—I think."

His smile morphed into a devious grin as his hands resumed squeezing her ass. He knew how to yank at her emotions like a yo-yo. She couldn't help but succumb to his bidding. Heaven only knew how much she wanted to experience his royal treatment again.

"Do you *really* have to leave so soon again?" she mumbled.

Smirking, he gave her ass a playful slap. Every inch of her body tingled with sensual delight.

"You really know how to lay it on me, don't you?" He stole another kiss as he unzipped his leather jacket.

She helped him along as he shrugged off the jacket and unbuttoned his jeans. Piece by piece, each article of their clothing was tossed to the floor until Gauge had her pinned against the living room wall, ravaging her body with his mouth. She was already wet for him.

His expert tongue swirled in her mouth, playing with hers. His taste was divine, sweeter and more addicting than any cake she'd ever made. He kissed down her neck while his expert hands moved along the contours of her hips. His tongue trailed down to her cleavage then flicked across each nipple. He greedily took one of her breasts in his mouth then sucked and slurped, moaning.

She cried out, her body responding immediately as both nipples puckered, becoming rock-hard. Her pussy clenched in pleasure, yearning to feel him inside her.

"Gauge… please," she whispered shakily.

With a wet pop, he released her breast from his mouth and looked at her with a dark gaze. He let out a low, animalistic growl and turned her toward the wall. She felt his hands splayed over her ass, and she braced herself on the wall. He grabbed her hips and, without warning, shoved into her pussy from behind.

She let out a cry of pain, and a sudden spark of pleasure overtook her body like wildfire. He consumed her, all of her. His thick cock completely overwhelmed her core. His breathing ragged, he moved in and out of her in a steady rhythm. Her heart pounding fast and furiously, she tried to move with him, but her lower half became numb from the pleasure. His animalistic growl continued, fiercer and stronger as he increased his speed. His hands moved back to her breasts. Squeezing two sizeable handfuls, he pushed deeper than he had before, almost past her limit. She didn't want him to stop, though. One of his hands teased her nipples while the other trailed down to the extra softness of her belly. It was strange yet alluring that her extra weight made him horny. The thought of a man like him loving her for who she was made her body feel hotter.

His breathing ragged, he quickened his thrusts. In and out he slammed his throbbing dick, the force of his weight keeping her pinned to the wall. She moaned louder, her eyes burning with tears of pleasure. Then the heat of her climax consumed her, the excitement overwhelming her brain, leaving her in a daze.

He shuddered behind her and came hard, filling her core and beyond. He let out a breath and remained inside her, still throbbing with the afterglow. He drew his hands around her midsection, gently massaging her pregnant bump.

"Our child…" he whispered then kissed down the contour of her neck.

Smiling, she closed her eyes and relished his gentle caress, a stark contrast from his rough fucking. His mood was as unpredictable as the wind, and she fucking loved it. Her walls tightened their viselike grip against his throbbing dick, yearning to milk him for more.

"You'll be a good father," she whispered back in a single breath.

He growled then bucked his hips against her, lodging his dick another inch deeper. "Damn right, I will."

She moaned in response to the sudden wave of pleasure that spread throughout her body. Then, unbidden, she came again.

"Damn, girl. You're so horny," he said.

She blushed. "I can't help that you do crazy things to me."

He chuckled and slowly pulled out of her. She felt his weight lift off her, and she slid to the floor, her wobbly legs too weak to hold her. He slid down with her and held out his arms to catch her. Aniyah's pussy ached, yet her insides felt so good. Breathing heavily, she rested the back of her head against the wall and stared at nothing in particular.

"Hey," Gauge said, "you all right?"

She grinned and slowly turned her head. "I've never felt better."

He snorted a laugh. "Good, then I hope you'll be ready to fight."

Fighting was the last thing she wanted to think about in the heat of that moment, but she knew it was important for him and their future. "I'll do what I can. I promise not to disappoint you."

He shook his head. "I know you won't. Aniyah Evans, you are the strongest, most determined woman I know, and I love you."

CHAPTER 12

Gauge couldn't take back those three words he'd told her. During the trip up to Greyson Creek, his mind repeated that moment over and over: *"I love you."* He'd never said those words to anyone before, and even he was surprised that he'd poured out his heart so willingly. The more he thought about it, the more he realized how scared he was—scared of losing everything if he failed, scared of losing *her*. And since he was about to be a father, even more was at stake. With too much to worry about, his mind felt conflicted.

During the trip, Aniyah hadn't acknowledged what he'd said to her. Instead, she'd asked about his family. He told her about everything, including the drama between his siblings, but he wondered if she even cared. The night before, when he told her he loved her, she'd simply smiled and kissed him. Maybe she was unsure as well. Maybe his words meant nothing to her.

He gripped the steering wheel, trying to get his mind off it. He had more important things to worry about, like saving his entire clan and his legacy. He wished he hadn't caved when Aniyah suggested they take her car. Gauge felt much calmer on his motorcycle. But they'd packed Aniyah's car with enough home-cooked food to last the clan a week. Gauge hoped to put an end to the war well before then, though. If he was lucky, perhaps he could end it in a single night.

During his time away, his clan mates and Axle had been training hard and preparing. After recently talking to Barron and giving him the latest update, Gauge hoped Barron would come through as he'd promised. The Blacktail Clan was a formidable family of bear shifters who occupied a high place in the shifter community's hierarchy. When he became best friends with Barron, Gauge would never have guessed it would turn out to be one of the greatest decisions he ever made.

Gauge arrived at Greyson Creek and turned down the inconspicuous dirt trail that led toward the cabin. He'd never driven a car through there, but the trees were cleared enough that a small one like Aniyah's could fit. They bumped and jostled about as he slowly navigated through the thick foliage. The area around them grew darker, the deeper into the forest they went.

"Where the hell are we going?" Aniyah asked.

"Home," Gauge replied, remaining focused on the bumpy trail ahead. Finally, he spotted the soft glow of lights from the cabin. When they were halfway there, Gauge saw two sets of glowing dots reflecting from the car's headlights. The dots scrambled away into the darkness.

Aniyah gasped. "What was that? More wolves?"

"No, some of my clan's patrols. They will come alert us if danger is near."

He drove to the cabin and parked out front. Before getting out, he placed a hand over Aniyah's. "I'll make sure none of the guys give you trouble."

She arched an eyebrow. "But aren't they your clan mates? Why would they give me trouble?"

"They've not been around a female in a long time."

"Really? Well, there's nothing a nice shiny metal bat won't fix." She reached in the back seat and pulled out a metal Slugger.

He laughed. "Damn, someone came prepared. But you'll never have a need for that while you're with me."

She smiled. "My knight in shining armor. I regret ever thinking chivalry was dead."

His heart swelled at her comment. Everything he did would always be for her. "It's not only about chivalry. It is my sworn duty to protect my mate at all costs."

They got out of the car and started unloading the food, then Gauge caught the scents of two of his clan mates. He looked up. One of them hopped down from the trees while the other approached from the shadows of the underbrush.

"Welcome back, boss," Dayton said.

The blond-haired, average-sized man had a surprisingly big heart. He could be as gentle as a kitten or as fierce as a clan of bears. Over the very short time Gauge had been around the rest of his new clan mates, he'd learned all about them.

Standing next to Dayton was Cory. Though he was the smallest member of the group, that didn't hinder his exceptional fighting ability.

Aniyah jumped and spun, facing the two men. "Whoa! Where did you guys come from?"

Cory cracked a smile. "Here, there."

Gauge acknowledged his clan mates. "This is my mate, Aniyah. Make her feel welcome. She is now a part of the family."

The two men nodded. Then Dayton said, "So glad Axle's stupid no-mate rule was redacted."

Gauge smirked. "You're welcome." He brushed past them and led Aniyah inside the cabin.

Inside, Weston was checking the windows carefully while Axle was in the common room, punching a canvas bag that hung from the ceiling. The furniture had been shoved aside against the wall, leaving a wide-open space for Axle to train.

Frowning, Gauge walked over to the bag and held it steady before it could sway back toward Axle.

Axle stopped in mid-punch and acknowledged Gauge with a start. "Oh, you're back. I'm ready to skin some wolves, since you don't trust me to patrol with the others."

"Because nobody wants to deal with your shit, Axle," Weston said, continuing to check the security of the windows.

Axle scowled at Weston then flicked his gaze at Gauge. "I still think we should take the fight to them."

"Nobody gives a shit what you think," Gauge said. "We've done it your way already. It sucked. I have a better plan. Just be ready when the time comes." He released the bag.

"Ehh…" Axle resumed punching the bag.

"All points of entry are secure," Weston reported, returning to them. "The enemy will have a hell of a time breaking through the reinforced glass."

Gauge nodded. "Call the others back from patrol."

Weston gave a mock salute and headed for the front door. He opened it, and Barron stood at the doorstep, flanked by Cory and Dayton, whose faces were pale. Weston regarded Barron with awe as the big man easily towered over him.

Gauge beamed at the sight of his best friend. "Barron! You made it!"

Barron cast a brief glance at the other clan mates and huffed. The others stepped aside to let him in. Weston left, gathering Dayton and Cory along the way. Barron and Gauge embraced briefly then bumped fists.

Axle stopped punching the bag and observed with a frown.

Barron scanned the room, his gaze pausing briefly on Axle and narrowing then returning to Gauge. "Nice place. It's as my parents described."

Gauge gave a hollow laugh then realized that was the first time Barron had been to the Whitetide Streak territory since Axle's takeover.

"So *you're* Barron Austin of the Blacktail Clan," Aniyah said, stepping closer to him and Gauge. "Gauge told me a lot about you."

Barron regarded Aniyah with a soft smile. "Good things, I hope." He turned toward Gauge and nodded. "You were right, man. She's a keeper."

Blushing, Aniyah playfully punched Gauge in the arm.

"Damn right, she is." Smiling sheepishly, Gauge wrapped an arm around her waist and pulled her close. "So? Are you guys in place?" he asked, acknowledging his clan mates again.

Barron shook his head. "Only six were willing to come. We're camped out not far from here."

Gauge deflated. "Only six of you guys? We're still outnumbered."

"I did my best. That's all my dad was willing to spare." Barron pointed at Axle, who was standing on a stepladder, unhooking the canvas bag from the ceiling. "Blame your lame-ass brother."

Axle paused and regarded Gauge and Barron with a scowl. "Shut the hell up, Barron."

Barron folded his arms, flexing his thick muscles. "Don't fuck with me, man."

Axle let the canvas bag drop. It landed with a loud thump. He hopped off the stepladder and stormed over to Barron, but Gauge put a hand to his chest, stopping him.

"Enough." He looked back at Barron. "Both of you. We can't change the past."

Part of him felt the urge to bite back those words, but it was too late. The idea of working with someone like Axle, who'd broken Gauge's trust, stung like hell, but in the short time since Gauge took on the role of alpha, he'd quickly learned that in desperate times, when his family's honor was at stake, there would be no enemies among his clan mates, only comrades in arms.

CHAPTER 13

ANIYAH COULDN'T BELIEVE THAT HER sweet, caring Gauge had such a raw past. Even when he told her all about his family's troubles, she hadn't realized just how horrible his situation had been. She couldn't imagine what being rejected by her own family and not being able to do anything about it would feel like. *Family—the ones you're supposed to love and trust.* Yet there she stood before two estranged brothers with two very opposing views.

The Whitetide Streak seemed more than welcoming of Aniyah, though being the only female was odd. Gauge had said Axle could never keep a mate and had disallowed the other clan members from mating as well. That must've been terrible for all the members, being banned from sex, love, and hope for a sustainable future for the clan. No wonder Axle was the most hated leader.

Axle leaned the heavy canvas punching bag against the wall in the corner of the common room. He took off his bag gloves and set them in a storage closet full of various sports equipment. She noticed a slightly pained look on his face. After learning about Axle's misdeeds, she had conflicting feelings about him. She wanted to feel sorry for Axle, but she also hated bullies and tyrants. Being a leader didn't mean being an asshole. She wondered if Axle had a story of his own that no one, not even his siblings, knew that had driven him to such action.

"Hey, Gauge," Barron said, sticking a thumb over his shoulder toward the front door. "The rest of my father's recruits are outside. Come meet them."

Gauge nodded at his friend then turned and stole a quick kiss from Aniyah's lips. "Be right back."

Aniyah flinched with a start and blushed. Gauge's wonderful taste invigorated her. "Okay."

Gauge flashed a glare at Axle then followed Barron out the front door.

After Gauge and Barron left, Axle grumbled under his breath as he dragged the pieces of furniture back to their respective places.

"So, you're Axle, huh?" Aniyah said, tilting her head.

He didn't look at her as he was fluffing and arranging the decorative pillows on the couch. "Yep. But don't talk to me. I don't want to deal with any more of Gauge's shit. He'll flip out and accuse me of trying to steal you away or something…"

Is Gauge really that extreme? "What do you mean? We've barely met, but I'd like to get to know more about the members of this clan if I'm going to be a part of it."

"I'm sure he's told you everything," Axle said flatly. Then he brushed past her and headed for the kitchen.

Aniyah followed. "He's told me how much he and others hate you."

"I did my duty, what I thought was right, for the good of the clan. Now I must live out the consequences of my actions." He pulled open the fridge and stared inside for a moment. "Want a beer?"

"No, thanks."

She paused and stared in awe at the large kitchen, big enough to prepare a meal for twenty people. It also sported all the latest and greatest appliances. A large, ten-seater dining table topped with a centerpiece of an overflowing assortment of fruit sat in an open space next to the kitchen. This was a heavenly place where Aniyah could see herself spending hours, letting her baking creativity fly free.

Axle grabbed a beer from the fridge, popped it open, and chugged half its contents in a few gulps. Then he retrieved a plate from a cabinet and a knife from a drawer and sat alone at the dining table with his back to her.

With a curious frown, Aniyah wandered over and sat across from him. "I get it. We all make mistakes. The main thing is that we learn from them."

He played with the knife in his hand, gently pressing a finger against the tip. "My mistakes cost the lives of new recruits. Cost my family's legacy. I destroyed all the things my aunt, the former matriarch, did for this clan."

Her gaze bounced from his face to the knife. She could sense the wheels turning in his head, but she wondered what he was intending. *That knife looks awfully sharp...* "Axle..." she said in a concerned voice.

"Hmm?" He glanced up at her as he stabbed the knife into the fruit bowl and skewered a fuzzy kiwi.

Aniyah's mouth opened in shock, then she relaxed and exhaled a deep sigh of relief. *Geez! Why did I assume the worst?*

Axle set the kiwi on the plate and retracted the knife. Then he picked the fruit up and used the knife to meticulously peel away its fuzzy skin. Afterward, he sliced the kiwi into six equal slices and laid them into a neat circle on the plate. He picked up a slice then slid the plate her way.

She glanced at the offering—so simple, yet a generous gesture from someone who'd been despised for so long. Part of her wondered if all that had happened was just a big misunderstanding. *Was he really responsible for the deaths of the recruits, or was he just blaming himself?* she wondered. "I'll respect your privacy if you don't want to talk about it," she said. Then she plucked a kiwi slice from the plate.

"There's nothing to talk about. I admit I fucked up. I'll be lucky if Gauge demotes me to the Omega position when all this is over."

She tilted her head, her brow scrunching. Gauge had begun to teach her about shifter society, though she still wasn't fully versed in the shifter ranks or their meanings. Based on Axle's tone, it sounded like the Omega position wasn't desirable.

"At least he hasn't banished you from the clan."

"Yet." Axle finished, taking another kiwi slice and popping it into his mouth. He appeared deep in thought for a moment as he chewed. Then he looked back at her. "Your heart is pure. Gauge did good, claiming you as a mate."

She let a small smile grace her lips. She hoped one day she would learn more about this gentler, humbler side of Axle. Her mind wandered about what her life might be like living among this tiger-shifter clan. The woods at Greyson Creek seemed spooky at night, yet they were peaceful. The cabin was in a perfect location to really get away from it all. Aniyah could definitely see herself living there with Gauge, away from the stresses of life in the city. Besides, she wasn't far from Ron's store, and there was, no doubt, a small town nearby where she could open her own bakery. If she stayed with Gauge, her dreams could very well become a reality.

The sound of furious scratching came from the front door, interrupting Aniyah's thoughts.

Axle, grumbling under his breath, stood up from the table, went to the front door, and answered it.

A large tiger stood on the stoop before him, its lush orange coat stained with blood.

Gauge and Barron, along with several other bears behind them, rushed to the stoop and observed the tiger.

The tiger growled at Gauge, causing him to start and look deeply contemplative about something.

"Shit!" Gauge rubbed his temples as though listening to something in his mind.

Barron's gaze bounced from Gauge to the tiger. "Is it time?" he asked his friend.

Gauge nodded. "Two Dessar wolves were spotted sneaking past the eastern marker."

"They're going to ambush—attack from all sides," Barron confirmed.

Aniyah bit her bottom lip, feeling the tension in the air rise. She was as ready as she was going to be to handle an ambush. "So where are we going first?"

Gauge looked her way. "You're staying here and defending the cabin. Weston will be here with you as well."

"Defend the cabin? That doesn't sound very exciting. Is that your way of saying 'stay here where it's safe'?" Fuming, she crossed her arms. "Don't treat me like some defenseless little flower. You said so yourself that you guys are outnumbered. You're going to need all the help you can get."

Gauge shook his head. "I've no doubt you can fight. But a shifter will overwhelm *any* human in close combat. I don't want you hurt. Besides all that, you are carrying our child."

She flared her nostrils in frustration. He was probably right, but she wasn't about to sit around and do nothing while Gauge was out there, fighting for his life. She was carrying their child, which made her all the more determined to fight for its future. If Gauge thought being human was a handicap that prevented her from defending the people she loved, she would prove otherwise. The night was not over yet.

CHAPTER 14

Gauge was unsure if the anxiety of the battle, bounding through the forest with Axle, or the thought of leaving his pregnant mate behind was making his heart pound incessantly fast. He didn't want to fight, but the madness needed to end.

"No wolf reaches the cabin," he'd instructed his clan and the Blacktail bears before they spread out to cover the perimeter. Gauge hoped their victory would solidify the Whitetide's territory in Greyson Creek.

He reached a clearing near the northeast perimeter and stopped. Axle followed suit. The smell of wolves was all around, very near.

Axle lowered himself to the ground, snarling toward an area of forest untouched by the moonlight. Six pairs of glowing yellow eyes appeared in the darkness.

A shiver ran down Gauge's spine. His ears flicked at the sounds of wolf howls and tiger roars from over a mile away, toward the southern perimeter.

"Six to two," Axle said in Gauge's mind.

Gauge looked at his brother. *"If you give a damn about the future of our family, you won't let those odds play with your head."* He tried to play it cool, but he knew the wolves probably already smelled his fear.

Axle grimaced. *"I'm not. Let's do this."*

The pack of wolves emerged from the darkness. Gauge and Axle stood back-to-back as the wolves encircled them. Gauge sized up each of the wolves and identified the largest one, the Dessar Alpha. *There he is…* He turned to Axle and projected, *"Zephyr is mine."*

Zephyr bared his teeth in a grim smile. *"These are the last breaths you'll take tonight,"* he said in Gauge's mind.

"We'll see about that," He revealed Xander Silverfang's ring hanging from his necklace.

The leader's eyes went saucer wide. Then he let out a terrifying howl. *"Y-You killed Xander! My brother!"*

"And you're next, asshole!" Gauge roared and leaped at Zephyr, his claws extended, and aimed for the wolf's throat.

Zephyr jumped out of the way and let out a terrifying howl.

The two other wolves suddenly pounced on Gauge, knocking him to the ground. Their combined weight on top of him crushed his energy. Pain shot through his neck as his skin fell victim to the wolf's jaws. He glimpsed the other wolf, who chomped down on his tail.

Gauge roared as endless pain surged through him.

It can't end like this. It won't…

Gritting his teeth, Gauge broke through the pain and groped the air for something solid. His claws penetrated one wolf's skull. He raked them down over the eyes then pushed. Howling in pain, the wolf immediately rolled off him. With less weight bearing down on him, Gauge rolled over, whipping his tail from the other wolf's mouth, leaving a tuft of his fur between its teeth. Still weakened, Gauge remained low to the ground while keeping his eye on the wolf and the leader, who stood strategically opposite him in a flanking position.

The wolf lackey charged at Gauge, snapping his jaws.

Gauge met him force for force, driving his claws into the wolf's chest. Using his own momentum, Gauge hurled the wolf into his injured comrade. Gauge shook the blood from his paws and faced the leader. He lurched his body forward in a feigning step.

Fortunately, the leader took the bait, sidestepping. Gauge swiped a bloody paw downward at the wolf's legs, attempting to flip him. One of Gauge's paws connected, but at the same time, he felt claws dig into his shoulder. They both tumbled to the ground, neither letting go of the other. The sensation of blood trickling from his shoulder wound made him cringe. He kept fighting, digging his claws into the leader's flesh without letting go, though the numbness in his shoulder intensified.

Zephyr rolled onto his back and used his hind legs to shove Gauge off. One claw from Zephyr's hind legs nearly took out Gauge's eye as it whisked across his cheek. Blood was no sooner trickling from the wound than Gauge leapt to his feet. *Damn.* Another scar that would never go away—another reminder of his failures.

The wolf jerked and scrambled about, his sharp movements causing Gauge's hold to slip from his jaws. The wolf struggled to his feet and lunged at Gauge. The impact sent them wrestling, pound for pound, on their hind legs.

Gauge spotted an old battle wound on the wolf's chest. The wolf's gray-white fur refused to cover the patch of open skin. That small weakness gave Gauge his second wind, and he used his weight to overpower the wolf, sending him teetering backward on his legs and falling over. Gauge stood over him, trapping the wolf where it had fallen. He sliced open the wolf's chest, using the wound as a guide. Howling, the wolf fought and kicked with the last of his energy, but Gauge continued eviscerating him. All he saw was red. The smell of blood burned his nose and riled his senses.

Exhaustion quickly set in once Gauge realized the wolf leader was dead. Gauge got off him and roared in victory. He looked over at Axle, who was facing off with the two last wolves after mauling one to its death. Axle was bleeding and limping. The wolves looked at Gauge then their defeated leader, and the hairs on their backs rose. They snarled and backed away from Gauge and Axle then turned tail and fled.

Axle growled after the escaping wolves and started to give chase, but Gauge called to him, *"Let them go."*

Axle looked back at Gauge. He set his paw down then yanked it back up again as if he'd stepped on something sharp. He let out a ragged breath.

Gauge spotted blood on his paw.

"We should… go after them," Axle said, clearly in pain.

Gauge approached his brother. *"Our clan mates will find them and make quick work of them."* He observed Axle's bloodied left-front paw. It was missing a toe. *"Holy shit. What happened?"*

Axle sat down and nursed his paw. *"One of those fuckers bit it off. I'll live."*

A growl rumbled in the back of Gauge's throat. He would ensure that Zephyr's corpse would serve as a warning to any other clan who dared challenge the Whitetide Streak. The Dessar pack, once the highest order of wolves in the region, had finally been defeated. *"Once word travels back to the rest of the Dessar pack about the death of their leader, they will all be done for."*

"*Does this mean this damned war is finally over?*" Axle asked.

Gauge exhaled. For the time being, he hoped so. With Axle no longer in power, the future looked a little brighter for the Whitetide Streak.

"*Maybe.*"

As his adrenaline subsided and calmness set in his mind, Gauge reflected on the battle, which he and Axle had fought together. If Diesel and Cammy had been with them, the family would have once again become united. But Diesel had made it clear that he wanted a new future for himself. And Cammy was her own woman, sworn to never get caught up in clan politics. As their big brother, Gauge respected their choice.

"*Let's head back to the cabin.*" As he grabbed the Dessar leader's corpse, something shiny slipped from the wolf's front paw. It rolled on the ground and landed in front of Gauge—a ring. Once worn by the Dessar's alpha, it was a symbol that solidified one's power. Few clans still practiced the somewhat older tradition, though it was mostly practiced by the wolves. Gauge brushed past Axle, dragging the leader along in his jaws back toward the cabin. "*Grab the ring. I have a better use for it now.*"

Chapter 15

ANIYAH STARED BLEARY-EYED AT THE clock. It was after midnight, and Gauge still hadn't returned. *Where* are *they? Did they succeed, or are they lying dead somewhere in the forest?* Fearing for their well-being while unable to do a damn thing about it was racking her nerves.

Weston had been patrolling throughout the house in his human form, stopping at every window. He had taken Gauge's orders seriously and hadn't allowed her to leave.

But how long are we supposed to wait? she wondered.

The cabin wasn't quite a mansion, but she loved its coziness. The living space was immaculate, with space for training, entertainment, and rooms used as sleeping quarters. Gauge had his own private floor upstairs, complete with all the amenities, including a kitchenette. While she adored what her future home offered, she could never enjoy it without the tiger-man she loved.

Weston returned to the living area and peered out the windows again.

"They're still not back," Aniyah said.

He moved to another window. "They will be. We just need to—" His body tensed.

Her stomach flipped. "What?"

He growled and leaned against the front door. "Two wolves approaching. Stay clear."

Sweat formed on her palms. *The wolves managed to break through their defenses? Does that mean Gauge is really dead?* Her heart dropped into her gut at the thought. She grabbed her metal Slugger, which had been sitting beside her duffel bag. Should the rest of the Dessar pack overtake the cabin, she would be ready to crack some wolf skulls. She would fight to her death just as Gauge had done.

A loud bang came from the front door, followed by another. Aniyah turned to see Weston struggling to keep the door shut. Even the reinforced door didn't seem to stop the persistent Dessar wolves.

Another bang and several scratches came from the other side of the door, and Weston shifted. Growling, he leaned up against the door again on his hind legs.

Aniyah gripped the bat's handle. The door shook, and she noticed a small hole in the wood. The wolf's scratching continued. She approached the door, and Weston roared at her. She froze, the fierceness of his voice sending a chill down her spine.

Another bang shook the door and tore it off its hinges in a splintered mess. Weston stumbled backward, and two large wolves appeared in the doorway.

Aniyah sucked in a breath. If either of the wolves got through Weston, she would hit a home run with their heads.

The wolves attacked Weston, piling on top of him, biting and clawing at him. Weston fought back, the muscles in his solid body flexing as the combined strength of the wolves overwhelmed him.

Aniyah took a step forward, poised to swing. One of the wolves noticed her and hopped off Weston. Crouching low, it slowly approached Aniyah.

Weston hurled the other wolf off himself and tackled him outside.

Aniyah faced the other wolf alone. She swallowed a lump in her throat. The wolf snarled, bearing a set of razor-sharp teeth. She took a step backward, white-knuckling the bat.

"C-C'mon, you son of a bitch," she muttered through clenched teeth. The thought of the wolf being the one responsible for Gauge's death made her blood boil, but she was prepared to join her mate with her last fighting breath.

For our child.

The wolf sank back a moment then leapt at her, its huge body barreling toward her like a boulder. She locked her gaze on the wolf's head and swung with all her might. A sharp pain surged through her arm when the bat made contact with the wolf's skull, and she dropped the bat. The wolf was knocked backward into the door frame. The beast let out a high-pitched scream as a jagged piece of wood impaled its neck. Blood spurted from the wound, then its body went limp.

Aniyah panted and stared wide-eyed at the wolf's corpse. Numbness overtook the pain in her right arm until she could no longer feel anything.

She clutched her arm, fearful that it might be broken.

Weston scrambled back inside, a bloody mess. Panting hard, he looked from Aniyah to the dead wolf impaled on the door frame. Snarling, he tore the corpse off the door and discarded it outside. Returning to Aniyah, he assumed his human form once more.

"Are you all right?" he asked in a gruff, animalistic growl.

Aniyah glanced at him, saw his naked, chiseled human body, and turned away, blushing. "Yeah, I'm fine. Just a little rattled—that's all."

The sounds of hurried footsteps approached the front door, followed by more animal snarls. She looked at the door, and two tigers limped in, one dragging a mutilated wolf's corpse.

Her stomach turned, and she covered her mouth.

The tiger dropped the corpse and shifted.

Aniyah gasped, relieved he was alive. "Gauge!"

Gauge acknowledged her then looked around the room. Seeing the broken door, he scowled. "What the hell happened in here?"

"We took care of a few stragglers," Weston said, buttoning a pair of jeans as he emerged from another room. He stopped before them and gawked at the corpse. "Holy shit—you killed Zephyr?"

"Yeah." Gauge nudged the wolf's head with his foot. "The Dessar won't threaten us again."

The other tiger limped over to Gauge and dropped something shiny in his hand. Then he limped off into another room.

"What's up with Axle?" Weston asked Gauge.

Gauge slipped the shiny object onto one of his fingers and shook his head. "He suffered a bad injury."

"I'll take care of him, man." Weston gave him a mock salute.

Gauge smiled slightly. "Thanks."

After Weston left, Gauge and Aniyah were finally alone. Aniyah looked down and rubbed her arm, her anxious, fast-beating heart finally slowing.

"Gauge, I was worried. Thank goodness you're all right," she said.

He sighed. "I didn't mean to worry you. It's been a shitty night for all of us." He walked over to the closet, grabbed a towel, and wrapped it around his waist.

"But we won, at least, right? You killed the leader?" She glanced sidelong at the corpse and made a face.

"Yes, and I'm gonna skin him and use him as a door decoration as a reminder to anyone else who tries to fuck with us. Are you all right?"

She smiled softly, but it quickly faded as she noticed the concerned look on his face. "My arm. It hurts."

Gauge examined her arm and hissed. "Damn it. I… I failed to keep you safe…"

Her smile returned, his deep concern warming her heart. "It's okay, Gauge. You fought bravely out there. You couldn't be in two places at once. It's not your fault. Besides, I'll be all right. But, holy shit, those wolves have thick skulls."

"Yeah, they do. I told you they were strong. What did you do?"

"I was helping to defend this cabin, like you said. They overwhelmed Weston, and one of them came after me. What kind of mate am I if I don't defend my home and my family?"

Gauge's hard expression softened. He carefully wrapped his arms around her and pulled her close. "Fucking hell, Aniyah. Did I mention you were amazing?"

Aniyah shivered as she was pressed against his naked body. Despite the pain in her arm, her legs quaked with need. She stared at his lips, longing to kiss them again.

He pulled her back and stared into her eyes. "I'll take care of that arm. But first, I want to give you this." He showed her the shiny object—a wooden ring with images of the moon phases etched around it. Spots of blood were present. "This is an alpha's ring," he explained. "It is a symbol of dominance, once worn by the Dessar leader. His death is proof of our victory. It is considered an honor in the shifter circle to gift an alpha ring to a mate. It symbolizes their bonding. It is an old tradition." He slipped the ring onto Aniyah's left finger.

Shock and awe overtook Aniyah as she stared at the ring. *A symbol of our bond.* Gauge's words were bringing hope for their future, unlike before, when he seemed so doubtful of himself. She adored the ring on her finger, the blood spots only adding a primal charm. Then she glanced at his necklace. "You have another ring?"

He inclined his head and grasped his necklace. "This one is personal, a victory I achieved where my brother failed. It is a reminder of why I am now the new alpha of the Whitetide Streak."

Smiling, Aniyah leaned in for a kiss. As they locked lips, her mind wandered, filling with thoughts about them. All she'd wanted was to live a simple life as a pastry chef, not to get caught up in shifter politics, fighting for her life.

This was much more than she'd bargained for, but she was totally there for it.

CHAPTER 16

GAUGE STRUGGLED TO NOT LOSE control of his tiger at the sheer anger of finding out that one of those damned Dessar wolves had injured her—and at the fact that he'd failed in his duties to protect his mate. Yet he was also impressed that she was willing to risk her life to fight for what was dear to her. Aniyah was strong and determined. He regretted ever doubting her.

While he was relieved the wolves were dealt with, the Whitetide victory was not without its consequences. When Barron and the rest of the Blacktail and Whitetide clans returned, he found most of them bloody, broken messes. Everyone was accounted for, except for Cory, who had sustained a fatal blow to his head and died in battle. They had barely escaped with their lives. Blaming Axle for everything would've been easy, but he no longer held the responsibility for the clan. Gauge had the Dessar leader's corpse skinned, branded with the Whitetide's tiger paw emblem, and posted conspicuously in front of the cabin for all to see and beware.

While his clan mates and allies sat around the main living area, nursing their wounds, Gauge headed upstairs with Aniyah and drew a bath with Epsom salts.

"Let me see that arm," Gauge said once Aniyah's dirty and blood-smeared clothes were tossed aside.

Wincing, she tried to move her arm. He examined it closely, running his hand down its length, feeling every muscle. Having had to tend to his clan mates' many battle injuries in the past, Gauge had little problem in determining Aniyah's issue.

"Yep, it's sprained," he finally said. "A good, hot bath will fix that."

Aniyah smiled at him. "Are you a doctor too?"

Gauge laughed. "Nah, but I've had sprains in every part of my body at some point, so I know what shit like that feels like."

She turned and entered the bath, wincing in pain. Once she was settled, Gauge climbed in behind her. His body was aching and bruised, but he trusted the bath would ease those pains. They soaked in the tub together, enjoying the ear-ringing silence after a harrowing night. He pulled her to him, resting her back against him, and sighed. Her soft, curvy body sank into him. He caressed her pregnant bump with his hands and smiled, reminded of his new alpha duties. In two more months, she would give birth. Unlike humans, the gestation period for tiger shifter children was about four months. But Gauge knew the day would come faster than a blink. During the time they were together, Gauge had helped educate and guide her along her new life, and she was prepared for what was to come.

His hard dick poked her in the ass, and she exhaled a soft moan. He wanted to fuck her in the tub. But the battle had exhausted him, and she was injured. He would make it up to her very soon.

He kissed the nape of her neck and muttered in her ear, "So, what do you think of my crazy family?"

She chuckled lightly. "'Crazy' is an understatement. But I'd like to think that there's never a dull moment with you guys."

"Yeah. It never used to be like this. I mean, there were at least other females."

"It does feel weird being the only female here, around a bunch of naked guys shifting into tigers."

He laughed. "Don't worry. They know you're off-limits. Besides, I encouraged them to go find their own mates."

Her smile broadened. "I'm happy to be a part of this clan."

He rubbed her shoulders, his heart fluttering in delight. "And I'm more than happy to have you a part of this clan too."

"And, Gauge…"

"Hmm?"

"I love you."

Holy fucking shit. He sucked in a breath. *Who knew those three words could be so powerful, especially coming from a woman like her?* "Really?"

"Really."

"Fuck, yes. I love you, too, Aniyah. More than anything. I can't wait to start our new future together with our new child. And I will get you your very own shop to make all the sweet things you want. You've already proven to me and everyone else here just how brave and strong you are. You may be the only female for now, but you've earned everyone's respect. Damn, who knew a pastry chef could be so deadly?"

She looked over her shoulder, smirking. "The sweetest desserts can be the deadliest."

His dick steeled. *Then fucking kill me now.*

EPILOGUE

Two months later…

GAUGE FLIPPED DOWN THE KICKSTAND and dismounted his motorcycle. He stood before a weathered brick building that housed a Laundromat, a pizza joint, an insurance agency, and a nondescript establishment on the end.

He furrowed his brow. *Is this the right place?* he wondered, remembering Cammy's clear directions. He was in the SoHo district, the eclectic part of New Rochford known for its specialty shops and upscale boutiques, loft-style art galleries, and cast-iron architecture. It was late afternoon, and the place was bustling with shoppers and locals walking to and fro. Gauge had never had a reason to go to that part of the city until then. He had to talk to Cammy face-to-face, but he'd let her choose the place.

His eyes cut to the nondescript unit, where an A-frame sign bearing a polyhedron image sat out front. *I thought she said we were meeting at a bar, not a fortune-telling place.* His curiosity piqued, he decided to investigate. He tugged on the door, which was open, and stepped inside.

The strong odor of hops immediately socked his senses as he entered the dimly lit establishment. He felt like he'd walked into a medieval fantasy world. Wood and stone dominated the walls, floor, and furniture, since the interior was designed as a fantasy-style tavern. Large chandeliers of fake burning candles hung from the ceiling's exposed wooden beams. More fake candles in wall sconces and standing candelabras provided a warm and cozy atmosphere. Tapestries bearing images of dragons, unicorns, and brave knights riding horses decorated the walls. But that was where the fantasy world ended. Regular people dressed in T-shirts, jeans, and sneakers sat at high tables and one large circular one, and some were gathered in an area with leather couches and chairs. Many were engaged in various types of board games, card games, and puzzles, while others enjoyed food and drinks.

"Over here, Furball!"

Gauge winced and followed his sister's strident voice. He spotted her sitting at a wooden two-seater table near a large bookcase filled with books and boxes of board games. He strode over and slid into the empty chair across from her. He could sense a drastic change in her demeanor, compared to when he'd last seen her several months before. She was in much higher spirits, no longer pissed at him. Perhaps being in this place—in her element—was what influenced her mood.

"'Bout time you showed up," Cammy said, smiling smugly. She picked up a tall, frothy glass of dark-brown liquid that smelled of licorice and ginger and took a sip.

Gauge gave the place another once-over. "What is this place?"

"It's called the Paisley Drake Tavern. It's a gaming bar, a place where us nerds hang out. My second home."

He wrinkled his nose. "A… gaming bar?"

"Yeah, y'know. You sit down, have a beer or two while you indulge in a board game. Or card game. Or you can hang out in the back room and play some video games on the giant, movie-theater-sized TV."

Gauge glanced at the patrons and suddenly felt incredibly out of place. Everyone was having fun, carefree, and not giving a fuck about what was going on outside in the real world. That was Cammy's vibe all the time. This was her world, and it felt totally foreign to him. "Well, I guess I should've known you'd choose a place like this to meet."

She arched an eyebrow. "What does *that* mean?"

"Nothing. Look, I just came to talk. I'll make it quick."

Cammy took another sip. "I'm listening."

When Gauge opened his mouth to begin, a guy dressed in a medieval-style tunic and breeches approached the table and set down a tray containing a massive salted pretzel hanging from a silver holder.

"Here you are, m'lady," the man said in a horrible faux English accent, casting a wide grin.

Gauge curled his lip at the stranger and growled, annoyed at the interruption.

Cammy's eyes lit up with delight. "Oooh! It's beautiful as always, Noah. I looove the pretzels here."

Noah, seemingly unfazed by Gauge's presence, turned his bright blue eyes toward Gauge. "And what can I get for you, good sir?"

"Get lost," Gauge muttered.

Cammy rolled her eyes. "Don't mind my simpleton brother. Get him a paisleybeer, whelp style. Oh, and he's *got* to try the troll balls." She giggled.

Noah snickered. "One whelp-style paisleybeer and one order of troll balls, coming up." He turned and left.

Gauge blinked several times. "What the hell? I'm not hungry."

"Fine—more for me. But I think you might like the troll balls, at least."

"Fuck that. I'm not eating anything called 'troll balls.'"

Cammy giggled. "That's just what it's called. But it's got all the stuff you love: beef, barbecue, pepper jack cheese, spinach, and all the herbs and spices you can imagine."

The combination of some of his favorite flavors teased his appetite. While he debated with himself, Cammy tore off a piece of the giant pretzel and popped it into her mouth.

"So, you wanted to tell me something?" she said.

He shook out of his thoughts and refocused. "Yeah. It's about—"

"Ooh!" Cammy popped up from the table, startling him. She slid out a box from the bookcase and set it on the table. Smirking deviously, she said to Gauge in a singsong voice, "Look what they have!"

Gauge sighed and flicked his gaze toward the box. Then his shoulders slumped. "Oh no… Not that. Anything but that!"

"That's right, Furball—*Baghchal*! And we're gonna play!" She opened the box and dumped the contents on the table.

Gauge groaned. That damned game, Baghchal—another childhood memory he wished he could forget. He and his siblings used to play it all the time. It was first introduced by their father, to help them learn strategy and the art of predator versus prey. Cammy was, naturally, unbeatable at the game and regularly spanked Gauge, Diesel, and Axle, no matter what side she played. Gauge was the worst player of his siblings, never being able to win a single game. But though his strategy skills were severely lacking in the game, he'd eventually mastered those skills in the real world. As a result, he swore to never subject himself to the endless torture of playing Baghchal against any of his siblings, especially Cammy.

"Can we *please* not play that fucking game?" he begged. "I'm trying to talk to you."

"We can talk and play," Cammy said, setting up the game. She laid out the cloth game board and tossed him a small velvet satchel containing more game pieces. "Here. You get to be the goat."

Gauge ground his teeth. "Hell no. I *always* have to be the damned goat. I get to be the tiger this time."

"Okay, how's this: if you beat me, you can be the tiger next time."

Gauge scowled. He knew full well Cammy wasn't going to show him any mercy. "For fuck's sake. Fine…" He gingerly reached into the satchel, pulled out a goat piece, and set it on the board.

Cammy's playful expression returned as she moved her tiger piece out from one of the corners of the game board.

"Will you *now* let me talk to you?" Gauge asked, setting down another goat piece.

"I told you I'm listening." She slid a tiger piece out of another corner.

Gauge set another goat piece down. As he opened his mouth to speak again, Noah returned with a tray of something that smelled heavenly. Noah set a plate of steaming hot meatballs and a glass of amber liquid in an empty spot on the table.

"One order of troll balls and whelp-style paisleybeer for the lady's simpleton brother." Grinning, Noah gave Gauge a sweeping bow.

Gauge growled at the happy waiter. "What the hell did you call me?"

"Cool it, Furball," Cammy said, not looking up from the game board. She slid one of the tiger pieces diagonally and jumped over one of his goats. "That was too easy," she said, swiping up the goat piece and setting it on her side of the board.

Gauge let out another growl of frustration. But that food smelled great. He was about to give the waiter a piece of his mind, but the man was already gone.

"Make a move, and try your troll balls." Cammy grinned.

He slammed another goat piece on the board, not giving a fuck where it was placed. "Look, Cammy. I have to tell you about what's going on at home."

"I left that life a long time ago. I don't care what's going on at home." She jumped another one of his goats, swiped up the piece, and tore off another piece of her pretzel.

"Would you care if I told you that Axle was no longer in charge?"

She paused in mid-chew. Her gaze swiveled toward him, and she swallowed. "You did it? You actually defeated him?"

He nodded and showed her his alpha's ring. "I had to defeat Xander Silverfang first to prove my worth, though."

Cammy's gaze flicked onto the ring then back to the game board. "Well, I'll be damned. So, you *do* have what it takes, after all."

"Would you consider coming back?"

She snorted. "Hell, no. I'm done with that life. Get it through your thick skull, Furball. I want nothing to do with clan politics. Besides, it doesn't matter who's in charge. They will never be Aunt Evaline."

Gauge swallowed a lump in his throat. No, he would never be their aunt, but that didn't mean he wouldn't carry on her ways and traditions. They had been branded in him since childhood. Unlike Axle, he never forgot.

"You're right. But I will do my best to uphold what she taught us."

"Try as you may, you are not her, nor will you ever be. Be your own man, Gauge. Rule with purpose. That is what she always told us. Your place is on the throne. My place is here." She made a fleeting gesture.

Gauge raised an eyebrow. "In a bar?"

"Damn right. This is my happy place. And when D's kids get older, I'll bring them here and teach them my ways. And make them badasses at Baghchal too." She smirked. "Speaking of which, hurry up and make your move."

He forced a small smile then stared at the game board. It wasn't looking too good for him, since she'd already taken two of his goat pieces. He took another goat piece from the velvet bag and set it on the board. "You're still taking care of his kids?"

"Ehh... I babysit from time to time. I'm the cool aunt. The kids love to play and have fun whenever I'm around. D can't stand it when we're having too much fun. He thinks I'm not teaching them basic life and survival skills. But honestly? The best life lessons are learned through play." She jumped another one of his goat pieces and swiped it up. "Geez, man, you suck."

Gauge ignored her jab and focused on her mention of Diesel. It seemed he'd opened himself up more to his family, even if it was just Cammy. Where their aunt Evaline was the glue that held the clan together, Cammy was the voice of reason that kept Gauge and his brothers in line.

"Like a well-oiled machine," their gearhead father would say amongst the rest of his cheesy, car-themed dad jokes.

"Well," Gauge said at last, "maybe one day, Kaylan will get to meet his cool aunt too."

Cammy slowly looked up from the game board. "Kaylan?"

"My heir."

She smirked. "Goodness, you've been busy, haven't you?"

"The last time I saw you, you put a fire under my ass, and I knew what I had to do." He paused, moistened his lips, and averted his gaze. "I guess... I should... thank you..." he muttered.

Her smirk turned more coy. "What was that?"

He shot her an annoyed look. "You heard me, brat..."

The afternoon continued as the two of them continued catching up on life. Gauge gobbled his troll balls, which ended up being one of the tastiest things he'd ever eaten, other than Aniyah's cooking. The pepper jack cheese–covered barbecue beef balls seasoned with herbs and spices melted on his tongue. And the drink—a licorice-flavored concoction of mixed ginger ale, rum, and root beer—added a perfect complement to his appetizer. Cammy knew him too well.

They ended up playing several games of Baghchal too. And Cammy's undefeated streak continued. But that time, Gauge didn't care. For the first time, after spending those moments with his sister, he felt closure at last.

THE END

About the Author

MARIE LONG is a novelist who enjoys the snowy weather, the mountains, and a cup of hot white chocolate. She's an avid supporter of literacy movements. To learn more about her, visit her website: www.marielongauthor.com.

www.ingramcontent.com/pod-product-compliance
Lightning Source LLC
Chambersburg PA
CBHW010751310726
48974CB00004B/879